Lyons caug of cordite

He reached back ... ...oft-soled shoes, Lyo... ...olt Python from his shoul...

He pointed first to himself, then at the door. Gadgets nodded. Kicking the door open, Lyons threw himself against the wall, waiting. Finally he peeked into the room.

Rosario Blancanales lay on the floor, his face bluish-gray, his chest and gut ripped open by point-blank shotgun blasts.

Lyons reeled back, his mind screaming: *The Politician's dead, he's dead.*

My friend is dead!

Mack Bolan's
ABLE TEAM

Mack Bolan's
PHOENIX FORCE

MACK BOLAN
The Executioner

Texas Showdown

Don Pendleton & Dick Stivers

A GOLD EAGLE BOOK FROM

WORLDWIDE

TORONTO · NEW YORK · LOS ANGELES · LONDON

First edition November 1982
Second printing December 1982

ISBN 0-373-61203-6

Special thanks and acknowledgement to Larry Powell
and L.R. Payne for their contributions to this work.

Printed in Canada

1

Jet blast tore at their clothes.

Carl Lyons cupped his hands over his ears, followed Gadgets Schwarz up the aluminum steps. An enlisted man ran after them with their overnight bags and the suitcase containing their weapons. Pausing in the jet's door, Lyons glanced back as the helicopter that had ferried them from Stony Man Farm in Virginia lifted from the concrete, the shriek of its rotors overwhelming even the roar of the USAF jet's engines. In seconds, the helicopter was lost in the night sky. Carl Lyons entered the jet. Another mission.

"Where to this time?" Gadgets asked Brognola.

"Bolivia." That good man Hal Brognola, now powerfully ensconced as Stony Man's White House liaison, had their briefing already prepared. He gave them folders with photos and typed sheets. Maps and grainy black-and-white aerial photos covered the conference table.

"Where's the Politician?" Lyons wanted to know. His blue eyes coolly observed the documentary data. His frame, robust like a veteran cop's but lean, youthful, was hunched as if in preparation for the action to come.

"Blancanales is already on his way. He was in the city, so we sent him on ahead while we assembled this information. He's better qualified to go in cold. At least in South America."

"What's going on there?" Lyons asked. He flipped through his information folder, saw maps of New Mexico, Texas, northern Mexico. "If we're going to Bolivia, why—"

"Who's this Monroe?" Gadgets held up a color photo of an elderly man in a suit ten years out of style. Airbrushing had added flesh-tone pink, but the old man's skin remained dead gray.

"You're going to Bolivia so that you can meet Mr. Monroe in Texas."

"Why don't we just go there straight?" Lyons queried impatiently.

"Two federal agents did exactly that. And now they're dead." Brognola glanced at his watch. "We have approximately fourteen hours until we arrive in La Paz. Read through the material. Prepare your questions."

"Who were the men who died?" Lyons asked.

"One was FBI. They found what was left of his body in a burned-out car. The next man was CIA. They found his body in a ditch. Death from exposure and sunstroke. Restraint marks on his wrists and ankles. He'd been staked out until he died, then dumped. But all of that is in your folders. Study the information. Your lives depend on it. You're the next men in."

Born the illegitimate son of a soldier and a West Virginia farmgirl, Tate Monroe went to Texas before he turned seventeen. Starting out as a laborer, he learned oil drilling and became a wildcatter. He earned his first million dollars in 1928, when he was almost twenty-one years old. Alarmed by the irrational economics of the late 1920s, he diversified into Latin American oil, minerals, and agriculture. The Great Depression multiplied his wealth.

He insured his Latin American holdings by investing in dictators. When political upheaval threatened his companies, he financed both the repression and the revolution, first buying the loyalty of the government in power, then, through a maze of false bank accounts and fictitious persons, buying the gratitude of all possible challengers to the government. Unverified reports alleged that Monroe often resorted to direct involvement to determine the future of small nations. The reports quoted second- and thirdhand stories of bribery, disappearance, assassination and atrocity. American agencies pursuing in-depth investigations lost contacts and agents. Mysterious fires destroyed records in agency offices, not only in Latin American countries but in Washington, D.C. Agency directors received warnings from congressmen and senators that if the agencies did not return their attention to the prosecution of criminals and communists, they risked severe cutbacks in funding. Investigations ended abruptly.

But he could not stop the nationalization of his Mexican oil fields in 1938. President of Mexico Lázaro Cardenas was not to be bribed. President

Cardenas refused to bow to Monroe's threats; he put the future of his nation above his own survival. Monroe could not get his assassins within range of the president before the brave Mexican completed the nationalization. And then Monroe could not take revenge: even if he could have killed President Cardenas, the assassination would not have regained Monroe's holdings; and further, the assassination would have risked war between Mexico and the United States, when the American government wanted Mexico as an ally against the European fascists. Secret memos revealed that only personal intervention by President Roosevelt and several senators convinced Monroe he would serve the interests of the United States and the Allies by accepting his Mexican losses.

But Monroe's compliance had a price. Unknown to the public and other defense industries, the War Department exempted Monroe's industries from competitive bidding. World War II made Tate Monroe a billionaire.

Newspaper and magazine writers created an American legend of Monroe's life. A poor boy who wrenched wealth from the Texas frontier by his own strength and daring made for sensational reading. As a man, his exploits filled the pages of the financial sections and the Hollywood gossip columns, as one day he led his workers to recapture a remote oilfield from communist revolutionaries, and the next day he took to bed an actress twenty years his junior. Heard in the rumor mills were the sounds of jazz and starlets' laughter in the primitive camps of his isolated enterprises. But there were other stories that would never appear in newspapers or magazines. Filed in locked cabinets of government agencies and the "Capitalist Atrocity" stacks of leftist agitators, these other stories detailed the annihilation of Indian tribes, spoke of "examples" made by chainsaw mutilation, "police actions" fought with Thompson submachine and Browning machine guns against machetes and rocks. The use of a "field-expedient" napalm—crude oil mixed with gasoline and dropped from a thousand feet in 50-gallon drums—became a standard device in Monroe's so-called Indigenous Education Program.

Then in the fifties and sixties, Monroe International was forced into retreat. Revolutions seized some operations. Dictators not content with bribes representing only one or two per cent of profits took one hundred per cent. But financial analysts knew that the single most significant cause mirrored the decline of the man Monroe. Earlier in his life, when an affair with an actress or model or singer took him away from his company, company profits leveled and exploration ceased. Monroe had no faith in underlings who could not equal his cunning and brutality, yet never trusted those who matched him. As his health failed—there was skin cancer, minor ailments, a major heart problem—his company operation withdrew to those sectors that could be managed by bank staff and accountants who never raised their voices in anger. Monroe lost his Latin American operations or leased them to the more dynamic multinationals.

He did not enjoy his retirement. His mind was twisted by age and medication, and Monroe ranted for hours about how his corporation's decline began in 1938, when politics stopped his attempt to retake the Mexican oilfields.

The United States government relaxed its surveillance of the aging oilman. Monroe was seemingly an old man near death. Newspapers did not even print his rantings anymore. He was no threat.

Until the news about the mercenary army.

"And that's when the FBI tried to slip a man in," Lyons commented. "They waited until the old creep had pulled in his horns, then tried to move a man in when it was already too late. Not smart."

"Why Bolivia?" Gadgets asked. "Monroe had some kind of operation going there?"

"Blancanales will brief us when we arrive," Brognola answered. "I think you two should get through the information here so you have time for some sleep. We have a full program for you after you leave La Paz—"

"Wait a second, Hal," Lyons interrupted. "Monroe's people have just offed an FBI man and a CIA man. He has people in the agencies, that's for sure."

"No. The agencies dropped several suspects. There's no chance there's—"

"No chance? Then what happened to the two Feds? One day they get the assignment, the next day they're dead. I want to know this: Who knows Blancanales is down there? And who knows about us?"

"No one knows. All of your team's operations are 'Top Secret.'"

Lyons looked over to Gadgets, held up a stack of forms. Each form had the photo and biographical details of an agent. Each form was stamped TOP SECRET. And at the bottom of every form, in red ink, were the notations: "Disappeared, presumed dead."

Passing the commercial airline terminals, the jet continued to the end of La Paz International's landing field. There, the military jet came to a stop among the parked aircraft of the Bolivian government and the official jets of the diplomatic community. As American Embassy personnel unloaded pouches and airfreight, Gadgets and Lyons, in military technicians' coveralls, slipped from the jet. Neither of them, bespectacled Gadgets least of all, looked like a soldier of Mack Bolan in such guise.

They carried their overnight bags into a hangar. Brognola followed a minute later in a pilot's uniform.

An airline-catering van took them from the airport. The local CIA station had prepared civilian clothes for them, including Kelvar bulletproof vests.

"What's the point with the vests?" Lyons protested. "Anyone serious will have an assault rifle or an Uzi."

"Part of the uniform," Brognola informed them. "Down here, all the businessmen and all their bodyguards wear them. Besides it gets cold at night."

"Which are we?" Gadgets asked. "Businessmen or—"

Brognola smiled. He handed them briefcases. Each contained an Uzi and several thirty-round magazines. "There's also a plate of Hotspur steel in the briefcases—"

Lyons tapped each of his Uzi mags to seat the cartridges. "A plate of what?"

"Hotspur steel plate. Konzaki called ahead and insisted on it. It'll stop all pistols, all fragmentation, and all standard auto-rifle rounds."

"Like this?" Gadgets held up the briefcase like a shield.

Lyons laughed. "Yeah, if you see a bullet coming, just quick fast block it. Uh-huh."

Brognola laughed, too. "You have something of Striker's sense of humor, Mr. Lyons."

The van lurched to a stop. The driver's voice announced: "Taxi waiting."

"Go, gentlemen. Straight out the back doors. I'll follow in another taxi."

"Where's Blancanales?" Lyons asked as he swung open the doors.

"He's there. Now go! No time for talk."

As they stepped from the van the brilliant afternoon sun blinded them. Blinking for a moment, Lyons looked around. They stood in the gutter of a narrow street. A few steps away, a taxi idled. At the corner of the block, two Indian women squatted against a pastel blue wall. A cast-iron pot boiled on a charcoal fire.

"Those Indians," Lyons marvelled. "They're wearing derby hats!"

Schwarz pulled Lyons to the taxi. "You heard the boss. Got no time to play tourist. Time to join up with the Political Man and get to work."

"But can you believe it? Derbies?"

Avoiding the city's boulevards, the taxi driver wove through the back streets of La Paz, slowing for buses and trucks, accelerating over cobblestones and potholes to race other taxis through the intersections. Soldiers marched on these streets.

Tires screeching, the taxi stopped.

"Adios," Gadgets said to the elderly Latin driver as they got out.

"And a good journey to you, men," the driver replied in bizarre Scottish-accented English. He pointed to an open shop door. "There be your address."

Then they stood alone in the street. The taxi screeched around the corner, disappeared into traffic. "Derbies and Scots," Gadgets laughed. "Bolivia's weird."

Stepping through the doorway, Lyons smelled the foul-sweet odor of excrement and blood and cordite. Death. He reached back to caution Gadgets, felt the muzzle of his companion's Uzi. Lyons slid the Colt Python from his shoulder holster, continued forward.

Past an entryway was a hallway. A skylight cast a soft yellow light on the polished linoleum. Lyons saw the doors to several rooms. All were closed, but a pattern of light marked one door and the hallway floor. Silent in his soft-soled shoes, Lyons moved closer.

He pointed to himself, pointed at the door. Gadgets nodded. Kicking the door open, Lyons threw himself against the wall, waited. He and Gadgets watched the other doors. Finally, Lyons peeked into the room.

Rosario Blancanales lay on the floor, his face bluish gray, his chest and gut ripped open by point-blank shotgun blasts.

2

The dim hallway spun around Carl Lyons. He staggered back, fell against the wall. He gripped his Colt, steadying himself as his mind screamed: The Politician's dead, he's dead. My friend's dead.

Gadgets leaned over the corpse, staring intently at Rosario Blancanales' face. He squatted down and turned the dead man's head to study the profile. He had to push hard to make the neck of the stiffening corpse turn.

"Schwarz!" Lyons was aghast.

"I don't know about this—" Gadgets answered.

"All I want to know is who did it." Lyons went to the corpse. A vast pool of dried, coagulated blood crusted the floor. Lyons looked down at the blood of his friend.

There was laughter behind him, gentle yet full-throated. And it was a laugh that he recognized. But it was the laugh of the person whose body lay blast-mangled on the floor. Lyons shook his head against the grief that twisted his thoughts. Then he saw Gadgets look up from the profile of the dead man. Lyons spun around.

"Nobody did it," Blancanales told him. "At least, nobody did me."

"You son of a bitch," Lyons hissed. He jammed his Colt into his shoulder holster, set down the briefcase he held.

"Sorry, bad joke, but we needed to test—"

Lyons drove a full-power karate kick into his friend's solar plexus. Blancanales side-stepped, simultaneously deflecting the kick and catching the punch Lyons threw. Blancanales clamped an arm around Lyons' throat, stopped the blond man's breathing.

"Really, we had to know if I could pass for him. Looks like I can."

Hal Brognola added: "Sorry, Lyons. Gadgets. We had to see what your first reactions were."

"You fooled me," Lyons gasped. "I thought it was you."

Blancanales smiled amiably. "It's good to know I'd be grieved for." His choke hold on Lyons became an abrazo, the strong hug of macho friendship Latin males share with one another. "Are you crying? Crying for me? Tough guy," Blancanales laughed. In his combat fatigues he looked casual, his confident maturity paradoxically youthful.

"Who's the dead one?" Gadgets asked. "And what's he got to do with us?"

"Pete Marchardo," Brognola said. "A violent life, in and out of scrapes since he was twelve. Rape, assault with a deadly weapon, armed robbery before he was eighteen. To escape the law he joined the marines, fought a few months in Vietnam before getting caught dealing drugs. He shot an M.P. He did time for that. After parole he passed himself off as a mercenary, specializing in international armed robbery. Then he drifted into the Caribbean drug world. He did a bit of work on the side last night, needed the money. He did an old routine on some new friends—that is, waving a pistol and taking the money. But it didn't work out. And those people don't call the police, they don't believe in due process.''

"Guess not," Gadgets commented, looking down at the remains of Pete Marchardo. Three point-blank shotgun blasts had ended his life. One had taken away his left arm above the elbow, the second had torn away a section of ribs. The third was a ragged two-inch-wide hole precisely through his heart: the coup de grace.

"So what's he got to do with us?" Gadgets repeated.

"He's our ticket to Texas," Blancanales replied.

Gadgets looked at Marchardo's face, then at Blancanales. "Might have to change your nose a little," he said. "Add a couple of scars." He looked at Brognola. "How did you...arrange this?"

"We didn't murder this man—" Brognola protested.

"It's more complicated than that," Blancanales explained. "The Feds have an informer in a gang. The informer gave us this information about Marchardo getting a Texas offer. So we hired Marchardo to bodyguard a drug shipment, so that we can watch him, monitor his phone conversations—"

"The Feds?" Lyons shook his head. "Now the Feds are running drugs? They need money that bad?"

"Lyons, it's a scam, honest," Brognola told him.

"Best way to know the trade is to get in the trade," Blancanales continued. "And it works out. Now we take the shipment north, Marchardo makes his connection in the Caribbean, and he—that's me—goes back to Texas with you two as the other two guys in the routine last night. Perfect."

"How well do people know Marchardo?" Gadgets asked Brognola. "The Pol looks like him, but does he sound like him? Does he act like him? If Marchardo has friends in Texas...."

"We don't know about the friends," Brognola admitted, "but the physical aspects are right. We intended to switch Blancanales for Marchardo, so we videotaped him, sound-taped him, everything."

"Do they know what happened?" Lyons pointed at the corpse. "I mean, he has friends there, and they're in mourning, and then the Man himself shows up...."

"That is one thing we're positive of," Brognola stressed. "No one knows of Mr. Marchardo's demise."

"Whoever had the shotgun knows," Lyons said.

"We already checked that. All he knows is that he killed a hood with a pistol. No one stayed around to check ID. No one knows Marchardo's dead. Positively no one."

"I hope so." Lyons looked down at the corpse. "Otherwise we will be positively dead."

"Nah," said Brognola softly. "The real danger is the Caribbean connection coming up. We got two agents in it already. You're gonna have to watch your pretty asses up there, all of you."

Jorge waited in the shadows of the doorway. He hoped the four men would leave the old house before the afternoon light faded. He already had photos of the four as they entered the La Paz house, but he wanted more. He had reloaded the camera so that the second set of photos would be on different negatives. It was important. It meant money.

Now that his fear had passed, he could think of the money. When the colonel called the night before with the orders, Jorge thought the job only routine. Wait in the doorway until men from a drug gang went to the house.... A simple job. Nothing difficult.

There had been a shooting at one in the morning. All the people on the street knew that. He bought that information when he arrived an hour later, though they would have told him for nothing. Then the waiting began. The night passed.

Would they return? He waited from two in the morning, shivering all through the night in the doorway. Day came and with it, fear. What if he had slept on his feet and not seen them? What if they had tricked him and gone over the roof? What if he had to tell the colonel that they did not return? The colonel did not like excuses. Soldiers who made excuses never became officers.

Now, he had a future. He had the photos. First, the two North Americans. Then the two who looked Mexican. Or Cuban. European? It did not matter.

He had the photos. Others would identify the gangsters.

But the second roll of film meant money. Perhaps enough for a motor scooter, or a television, perhaps a new parade uniform.

Voices! Jorge braced his shoulder against the wall and found the opposite doorway through the viewfinder. He pressed himself far back in the doorway, waiting until the first North American appeared.

The motorized 35mm camera caught the gangsters as they emerged. Full face, profiles, hand gestures, each man with the others in a group. Jorge took thirty-six exposures in a minute. Then the men got into a chauffeured limousine.

As the black Mercedes pulled away, Jorge leaned out for a last shot. He wanted the limousine's license number. But he had no more exposures in the camera.

Too bad. At least he had two sets of photos. One for his colonel, the second for the feared El Negro, warlord of the cocaine armies. El Negro paid very well and remembered those who helped him.

And who knows, Jorge thought as he walked to the boulevard, perhaps the colonel might fall from grace with the government. Perhaps the government would restore El Negro's rank and position. Jorge could be an officer to any colonel....

Running his hands over the leather upholstery of the Mercedes limousine, Gadgets commented: "Nice car. Government workers have it made down here."

"This car isn't government." Brognola pushed a

button, opened the limo's bar. He took orange juice from the tiny refrigerator. "It's one of our gang's cars. They use it to—"

"The United States government bought this monster?" Lyons looked around the leather and rosewood interior. "Someone's got new ideas about law enforcement."

"Actually, I saw in the report that they traded several kilograms of cocaine for it. So there was no expense to the taxpayer." Brognola held out crystal wineglasses to the others, offered them orange juice. Lyons pushed his away; Brognola smiled. "And then when the trader went North, they tipped the Colombian authorities. And the Colombians took him. Again, at no expense to the American taxpayer."

Lyons laughed. "That's more like it. Cost-efficient law enforcement." He took a crystal glass, poured orange juice for himself. "Plus fringe benefits."

"Enjoy it quickly," Brognola told him. He glanced outside as they approached the metropolitan center of La Paz. "You start work in a minute."

"What are we doing?" Lyons asked.

"You have the identity we prepared. You're the world-weary mercenary. The good soldier who came home from the war, found your wife and the town mayor in bed, killed the mayor. You've been running ever since, one false name after another. And you, Schwarz—"

"—Suspected of killing my superior officer in Vietnam, hounded from job to job by federal investigators until I finally skipped the country," Gadgets recited.

"And I'm Pete Marchardo, international punk," added Blancanales.

The limousine slowed to a stop. They peered outside, saw modern office buildings, crowded sidewalks, shop windows displaying European fashions. The chauffeur left the driver's seat and walked two steps to a waiting taxi. The taxi sped into traffic.

"Speaking of Marchardo," said Lyons suddenly, "what happens with his body? We can't have him being claimed by his relatives."

"He got a thermite cremation two minutes after we left." Brognola pointed to the driver's compartment. "Up front, Lyons. Time to work."

"I'm driving? I don't know the laws here—"

"Standard limousine routine," Blancanales answered. "You own the road."

"See you, Able Team, in a few weeks." Then Brognola stepped out and immediately merged with the afternoon crowd.

"So be it," Lyons commented as he took the wheel. He found the switches of the German luxury car. He flipped the intercom switch. "Where to?"

Tapping on the window of the closed photography shop, Jorge got the attention of the owner, Señor Brillas. The elderly man waved him away. Jorge beat on the window with the film canister. Angry, Señor Brillas shuffled to the door, pointed to the "Closed" sign. Then he recognized Jorge. He opened the door for the young man. He knew why Jorge was there.

"This is for El—"

"Silence, boy!" Señor Brillas glanced in both directions, saw no one out of the ordinary on the narrow street of shop fronts and apartments. He clutched at the youth and pulled him inside.

"What do you have for him?" The old man would not mouth the warlord's name.

"This." Jorge held up the can holding the roll of 35mm film. "Photos of North Americans. They went to a place where—"

Hands like bare bones clutched the film, then pushed him out the door. "It is not important I know. I will send the photos to him. You give him the information."

Leaning in on the door as the old man tried to close it, Jorge warned him: "No mistakes! This is life and death!"

Señor Brillas locked the door. He turned the small film canister in his hands. "Soldiers, cocaine, and death. Always."

From a nearby café's pay phone, Jorge called Zavala, lieutenant to El Negro. The chatter and laughter of four teenage girls forced Jorge to put his other hand over his free ear and speak closely into the mouthpiece.

"This is your friend with a camera. Can we speak?"

"Why did you not call this morning? What do you have to tell me?"

"They did not come until only an hour ago. I have photos of all of them."

"And names? What gang?"

"They were North Americans. Two of them. Perhaps the others. You will have the photos soon. You will see.''

''Did they take the dead one with them?''

''No. They left him. And they laughed when they left.''

''Did they look like DEA?''

''I don't know. They wore suits. Three of them looked like soldiers. What I say means nothing. You will have the photos. There is nothing else I know.''

''Thank you, friend. You will have your money soon. And soon we will know who those Americans are.''

Slamming down the telephone, Jorge laughed out loud, slapped his hands together. What did he want most? An Italian motor scooter? Or a new uniform? Then it occurred to him. If the Americans were agents of the Drug Enforcement Agency, perhaps El Negro would give him even more. He could have both the scooter and the uniform! Jorge would be the envy of the barracks.

Following the directions Blancanales gave through the intercom, Lyons eased through the bumper-to-bumper traffic. Whenever the other drivers saw the limousine, they eased away.

''Marvellous how a hundred-thousand-dollar car cuts through traffic jams,'' Lyons told the others through the intercom.

Gadgets smiled wearily. ''We're going about five miles per hour.''

''They're all making room for me. I feel like the king of the road.''

Blancanales laughed. "It's not the car, it's who they think is inside it. Pull over in front of the hotel there."

As Lyons coasted to a stop in front of the doorman, two soldiers in combat gear saw the limo, snapped to attention. Once Blancanales and Gadgets appeared from within the limousine, the soldiers relaxed. Lyons started out of the driver's door. Blancanales leaned over the roof of the Mercedes.

"It's the custom here for the driver to stay in the car and keep the engine running. Things happen fast. Stand by while we go in and get our gangsters."

Lyons waited, switched on the radio. He watched the traffic pass. He glanced in the rearview mirror. He wanted to put the Uzi on the seat beside him, but he was uncertain how the soldiers or the local law enforcement would react to an automatic weapon in a civilian limousine. So he snapped open the briefcase latches, then kept his hand on the grip of the Uzi. On the radio, a man's voice ranted and shrieked. Lyons did not know enough Spanish to understand what was said, but when the raving went on for minutes, without other voices or commercials, he spun the dial. "Politics or religion," he muttered. "Got to be."

The voice blasted from all the other channels. Lyons turned off the radio. "Politics."

Then he saw Blancanales and Gadgets escorting a man and a woman toward the curb. They were the agents who were setting up the Caribbean connection. The man was middle-aged, paunchy, wearing a conservative gray suit. The woman, tall and lithe, young, wore red satin and a black mink. She looked like sin striding.

Lyons watched her strut to the limo, the satin of her gown flashing with each step as the shimmering fabric revealed the curves of her hips and thighs.

Texas could wait. Lyons turned in the seat, watched through the Plexiglas partition as she swept into the Mercedes, her lovely features framed in mink and flowing black hair. Diamond flashes punctuated her profile. She hit the intercom button, commanded:

"To the airport!"

3

Through the ten-power optics of the binoculars, Lyons followed the lines of Flor's thighs to the flawless coffee-colored swells of her buttocks, then to the arch of the small of her back. Fifty feet from where he hung by a safety strap in the yacht's rigging, Flor Trujillo sunbathed nude on the forward-most deck. She turned. Lyons inched the binoculars over her body, from her thigh to the curve of her waist, to the lines of her ribs. She leaned on one elbow while he studied her breasts. They were oiled, perfect. The pattern of her towel was reflected in the shiny half-dome of one breast's underside. The nipple, coffee-berry red, rose from her flesh even as he watched, and stood erect.

He focused on her face. Her eyes startled him. They fixed him, returning his stare. Her lips mouthed words, slowly, distinctly, so that he could lip-read:

"Fuck off, asshole."

Lyons laughed, waved, returned to scanning the horizon. The azure calm of the Caribbean extended to all the horizons. An hour before, he'd seen the smudge of diesel smoke to the east. The touch of gray had faded without the ship itself appearing. Now he scanned an utterly empty Caribbean, the expanse of ocean enormous, the horizon visibly curved, the far distance lifting like a breast to a thirsty blue sky.

He returned the binoculars to Flor. She lay on her back, sunglasses shielding her eyes, casually flicking water from a dish over her body to cool herself. The water beaded like blue jewels on the coffee of her skin.

Sweat ran from the cotton gloves that Lyons wore. During his first hour on watch, his hands had turned red from the sun. Now he wore the gloves, a long-sleeve shirt, cotton pants, a kerchief over the back of his neck, and a wide-brimmed straw hat. Sweat dripped from his body, but not only from the tropical heat. His hand-radio buzzed:

"See anything?" Blancanales asked.

"Lots of ocean. Nothing on it except us."

"What do you think of Flor?"

"Torture. Can you see her?"

"She walked through in her robe. She doesn't need to be naked to make a heat wave."

"Speaking of heat waves, what the hell am I up here for? We got radar."

Gadgets' voice came on. "Stealth technology, man. These dope navies don't have to go to congress for the latest stuff. They got the cash, they get the equipment. That makes them potentially superior."

"So you come up here and get fried."

"Okay, take a break, Lyons," Blancanales said. "I'll take an hour with the glasses. Could be interesting...."

In thirty seconds, Lyons stepped into the air-conditioned semidarkness of the bridge. Gadgets sat at the radar console, glancing to the screen's phosphorescent green sweeps as he read an XM-174 instruction manual. The weapon itself lay in pieces on the console. A case of 40mm grenades sat on the floor. Someone had scrawled on the side of the crate: "Frag/W. P./Conc."

"You be careful with that stuff," Lyons cautioned. "You sink this boat, it's a long swim to shore. We don't even need the heavy weapons, right? Tonight's just a make-believe, I thought."

Blancanales took the binoculars. "Boy Scout motto—"

"—Be prepared, huh? See you in an hour, Pol. I'm going to hit that cold shower."

Stripping off his sweat-soaked clothes as he walked through the brass and teakwood passage, Lyons shoved open the door to his stateroom, where he threw down his clothes and stepped into the shower.

The cold water felt like ice. For minutes he stood under the shower stream, his eyes closed, letting the chill water wash over his face and body. Only when he began to shiver did he reach for the towel.

Flor put the towel in his hand. He started back, reflexively. "Don't be afraid," she taunted. "I'm only looking. And you don't look too bad, considering the bullet damage."

He ran the towel over the welt of scar on his ribs. It hurt when he touched it. Sometimes he dreamed of looking down the barrel of the M-60 that had come within an inch of killing him on Santa Catalina Island. He continued drying himself. "I got the impression you thought staring was impolite."

"Impolite and counterproductive. Why'd you take the cold shower? Is it hot up there?"

He nodded. She wore a white canvas beach robe. She came close to him, dabbed at the cold water on his face and throat. Under her robe she wore nothing. Her body smelled of coconut oil.

"You know the worst part of this work?" she asked him. Lyons shook his head, no. "It's the boredom. When there's action, I'm too busy to think. But when I'm bored, I can't stop thinking. Come on," she said, as he smiled at her slightly. "We've got fifty-two minutes before you go back on watch."

Light from the radar screen cast patterns of green on Gadgets' face. The high-speed scans revealed several ships in the distance. He lifted the hand-radio to his lips:

"Political Man in the Sky, you see any lights to the south or west?"

Thirty feet above the deck, Blancanales swept the night horizon with the binoculars. The Caribbean shimmered under a sliver of moon and the vast swirls of stars. From time to time a meteor scratched the night sky.

"Nothing in those directions. But I've got some lights to the east."

"Watch for anything unusual. The radar shows four ships between us and the mainland."

"Running without lights? Dopers."

"There's three navies operating dope patrols out here. Could be anyone. Keep watching."

Lyons leaned over Gadgets' shoulder, studied the blips. "Which one is the freighter?"

"Maybe this one," Gadgets pointed. "Or maybe this one."

"And the Colombian cutter?"

Gadgets grinned, pointed to the same two blips. "Or maybe the other one."

"Could be anyone out there, right? Good guys, bad guys—"

"Tourists, UFO's, ghost ships. And mucho dopos."

"What happens if they've got that stealth technology you talked about?"

"Then they don't show up on the screen. Lyons, my friend, why don't you go load magazines? Shoot at the moon, anything. You're making me nervous."

"You're nervous? This whole scene's got me twitching—"

Footsteps and Spanish conversation interrupted Lyons. The make-believe Señor and Señora Meza entered the control room. They both wore denim jump suits. Flor wore a black nylon windbreaker also. In their dark clothes, the undercover agents would make very difficult targets.

Even dressed for battle, Flor was lovely. Lyons just couldn't take his eyes off her.

"Are you three ready?" she asked.

"Hope so," Gadgets told her. Lyons only nodded.

She glanced at her watch, then leaned over the radar screen. "Contact in thirty minutes," she announced. "Remember, our plane will come while we count out the cash on the freighter. When we ignore their commands and attempt to flee, they'll rocket the freighter. Please, do not become confused and go to the wrong side of the freighter. The plane will strafe and rocket one side repeatedly. If—"

"I got it," Gadgets interrupted. "I know the routine."

"When I came in, you two were talking of nervousness. There can be no mistakes."

Gadgets pointed at Lyons, laughing. "That's the man with the nerves."

Lyons massaged the long scar from the .308 slug.

Flor smiled. "Try not to think about it."

Without further words, Flor and Señor Meza left the control room. Gadgets continued studying the radar screen.

"There's a blip here that bothers me. It's the size of a freighter, but it's moving too fast. Strangest thing."

"Don't even tell me about it." Lyons slung the XM-174 grenade launcher over his shoulder, let it hang by its strap. He took an M-16, checked the tape that bound the two thirty-round magazines end to end. Then he buckled a web belt of magazine pouches around his waist.

Gadgets looked at all the armament. "All right, peace through superior firepower. Twenty eight minutes until whatever."

Lyons went out to the night to wait.

Rotor-throb descended from the stars. High above the yacht's deck, Blancanales leaned back against the safety strap and quickly swept the sky with the binoculars. He found a black silhouette. Even as he keyed his hand-radio, Gadgets' voice boomed over the yacht's loudspeakers:

"Gentlemen, this is most definitely an unexpected event. Repeat, this is Number Ten. Number Ten."

Flashes on the horizon caught Blancanales' attention. He focused on the southern horizon, saw red tracers stream from the distant sky. Dashes of red and orange tracers arced upward, then one more flash revealed the deck and superstructure of a freighter. The scene became as bright as midday as a magnesium flare floated down on a parachute.

The white light glinted off of the wings of a prop-plane.

"Oh, shit," Blancanales muttered. "Somebody screwed up." His hand-radio buzzed. Lyons' voice came on:

"What's going on?"

"Mucho problemas."

Like a jackhammer on steel, the sound of tracers raking the deck of the freighter banged alongside the yacht. Ricochets buzzed in all directions, some invisible, others searing red. Blancanales watched lines of tracers shoot from the silhouette of the helicopter above them. Then the gunner targeted the yacht.

A long burst ripped the length of Able Team's sailing vessel. Blancanales watched the curtain of red phosphorescent tracers pass within an arm's reach of him. The roar of the passing slugs was an unforgettable sound. The wooden mast he was hanging from bucked and shuddered with the impacts of slugs. His hand radio buzzed again. Lyons yelled:

"Get out of there! That stuff passed so close it lit you up."

Scrambling down the mast's ladder, Blancanales did not stop to answer his comrade-in-arms. Only when his boots hit the deck did he key his hand-radio.

"I'm down. Where are the Mezas? We gotta get out of here!"

Shouting came from the deck of the looming freighter. Fifteen feet above where Lyons stood, he saw a man brace a weapon on the freighter's railing and fire at the helicopter. It was a belt-felt machine gun. Brass showered down on Lyons. He saw a line of tracers cross the fuselage of the helicopter.

The rotor-noise deafened Lyons as he ran to the rear to identify the freighter's boarding ramp. He crouched as the helicopter's door gunner sought out the machine gun on the freighter's deck. Tracers sparked in the shadows.

Xenon light revealed the machine gunner on deck. He lifted the heavy weapon and fired from the hip. Tracers crisscrossed. The xenon beam died as slugs slammed into the helicopter. Then the machine gunner died, a stream of tracers from the helicopter finding him and slamming him back against the railing. Lyons watched the slugs rip through the man's body, tracers blazing through him to punch into the yacht's deck. Burst after burst hit the dead man.

"We must board now," Flor called urgently to Lyons. She hurried up the ramp, a CAR-15 in one hand, a satchel in the other. She had the collar of her jacket turned up. The copter was gone.

The boarding was hasty, uneventful. The business was accomplished wordlessly, in a silence blessedly rotor-free.

The uninvited helicopter was surely the work of the two hoods stung by the real, but late, Marchardo. To ensure the end of the deal. All it had succeeded in doing was scare away the attack plane.

The buglike menace roared in again from the freighter as the two merc agents emerged at the top of the ramp. It sped over the ship.

Flor led the descent to the yacht, followed by Señor Meza and three other men. Two were in suits, one in a leather Eisenhower jacket and carrying a Thompson.

Señor Meza checked over his shoulder as the helicopter veered away, circling the ships.

"These men are your link with a Mr. Pardee," Flor told Lyons as she passed, nodding toward the others. "Wait until we cast off from the freighter before dealing with the helicopter."

Lyons laughed cynically. He saluted Flor. "Yes, ma'am! Anything you say!"

"Don't sweat it, Ironman," Blancanales said beside Lyons. "It's only air holding that thing up...."

Able Team followed the others to the bridge as the yacht cast off. Flor and Señor Meza leaned over the radar screen while Gadgets took the ship's wheel. The other three gangsters peered through the windows, looking for the helicopter. Lyons shouted:

"I suggest you all get below—"

Blancanales cut him off, repeated the words in

Spanish. Tracers ended all discussion. Streaks of red shattered the windows. Glass showered the gangsters and Señor Meza as they scrambled down the stairs. Flor raised her CAR.

Lyons jerked her down. She fell in the broken glass, tried to shove him away. Slugs slammed into the bridge again. Flor lurched.

"You're hit!" grunted Lyons.

Silence. Then they heard the helicopter circling. Its gun fired on the freighter again. Flor groaned, sucked down a breath. Lyons slipped his hands under her jacket and searched for the wound.

"Get the helicopter!" Gadgets shouted. "I'll take care of her."

"Let's go!" Blancanales dragged Lyons away from the woman, pushed him through the door. "Wait until they come back, then pop them." Blancanales pointed to the XM-174 grenade launcher that Lyons carried with the M-16.

"I'm not waiting!" Lyons fumbled through the magazine pouches around his waist, seeking the magazine tagged with textured tape. He dropped the magazine from his M-16 and jammed in the tagged mag. "Come and get me, fly-boys!"

Popping single shots, Lyons sent tiny tracers at the helicopter. When he got the range, he fired bursts, the tracers arcing into the distance. The helicopter broke away from the freighter and crossed in an instant the three hundred yards that separated the ships.

"That got their attention." Lyons slung the M-16 over his back, then took the XM-174 in his hands and released the safety as he climbed to the top of the bridge housing. The helicopter swooped in at water level, raking the deck of the yacht with more machine-gun fire. Lyons waited.

The helicopter then paused, hovering only a few feet from the deck railing. Lyons saw the face of the door gunner over the grenade launcher's sight as he squeezed off the first 40mm round. The upper half of the gunner's body disappeared in a flash of light. Lyons fired round after round into the interior of the helicopter—fragmentation, concussion, white phosphorous, fragmentation again.

Veering straight up, the helicopter pilot tried to gain altitude. Lyons continued firing, blowing away a pontoon, spraying the ocean with streamers of white phosphorous. Then a blast, a series of blasts, a boiling explosion as the copter was blown apart into a crackling cascade of hot fragments and phosphorous rain. Shards of wreckage showered the sea.

"Great shooting!" Gadgets Schwarz nodded to Lyons as he returned to the bridge. Squatting amidst broken glass and weapons, Gadgets was fumbling with Flor's nylon jacket as the woman sat in the captain's chair, holding a frosty beer can against her shoulder.

"I thought you were hit...." Lyons started.

"I was—"

"With this." Gadgets pulled a flattened slug from the jacket's fabric. "She's wearing a Kelvar windbreaker. Neat, huh?"

Glancing outside, Lyons saw several bullet holes through the brass railing that encircled the bridge deck. The bullets had drilled through the brass, then the teakwood exterior, and finally through the interior's teakwood paneling.

Flor popped the top of the beer, gulped.

"You are one lucky woman," Lyons told her.

Foam spilling down her face and onto her chest, she offered the beer to Carl Lyons, saying:

"Very lucky. There's nineteen hours and thirty minutes until we dock in Jamaica."

4

Back in La Paz, ex-Lieutenant Navarro spread out the photos of the North Americans on his desk top. First, he arranged the thirty-six exposures in chronological order, referring to the negative to confirm the correct sequence. He numbered the photos. He studied the exposures, looking for the sub-sequences within the thirty-six. He knew the surveillance agent had used a motorized camera. Intervals of only a second separated some photos. A pause of seconds separated other photos.

He divided the photos into four groups. Each group represented bursts of exposures. The agent had simply focused on the moving subjects and held down the trigger-button. The sequences allowed Navarro to observe the interaction of the four men, as if he watched four film clips.

Though two of the men could possibly be Central or South American, they did not exhibit any distinctive mannerisms: they did not have the expressive hand gestures of Mexicans or South Americans, nor did they wear the scowling features of ex-military officers. The other two looked North American: light hair, fair skin, quick smiles. Navarro did not believe they were European—they did not show English re-

serve, French gestures, German mannerisms—but he
knew he could be wrong.

One thing puzzled Navarro: though three of the
men often turned to the fourth as if he were their
leader, they did not defer to him. They did not sur-
round him like bodyguards. They did not walk close
to him, as junior associates would. And he was not
their prisoner. They joked with him, questioned him.
One of the photos showed the blond man pointing a
finger at the apparent leader as if the North
American was threatening him. But in the next exposure, approximately two seconds later, the four
men laughed.

Without knowing the identities and roles of the
four men, Navarro could not interpret their actions
in that scene. He selected several of the photos for
blow-up.

Today, he would ask El Negro for authorization to
post agents outside the Drug Enforcement Agency
offices. Those agents would watch for the four men
in the photos.

There was another way to gain the identities of the
four men. Navarro knew an expatriate American
who recruited guards and soldiers for exiled conservative politicians and retired military officers. The
Yankee boasted that he knew "every American mercenary south of the Rio Grande."

Navarro would test the Yankee.

Neon flashed behind longhorn skulls. Wagon wheels,
frayed leather horse collars, Mexican blankets,
weathered ranch tools hung on the mirrored walls.

Strips of red, white, and green bunting—the colors of the Texas flag—trimmed the black plastic bar and the chrome of the stage. Jamaica, too, was weird.

European tourists in designer jeans and Hawaiian shirts hustled the black waitresses. A Jamaican woman in an Annie Oakley buckskin dress shrieked, fired a six-gun cap pistol.

Three young Jamaican men in black slacks and white shirts and ties watched the tourists and re-splendent Jamaican cowboys and cowgirls. The red blazers hanging on the backs of their chairs identified the young men as workers from a nearby hotel. An immaculate black cowboy passed the three hotel workers, the cowboy's high-heeled lizardskin boots and tailored jeans giving him the mincing steps of a debutante. The workers looked to one another and laughed. Soon they paid for their beers and left.

Craig Pardee came through the backstage door. He came to the table where Blancanales—a.k.a. Pete Marchardo—waited. Pardee signaled for two beers before he sat down.

"My girl's got the stage jitters," he told Blancanales. "She don't usually sing country, but it's the only work she can get. They hired her 'cause she's got a Texas accent. This country-and-western fad, you know. Told her I'd take care of her, give her the high life while I did my business, but she says she's got to work. Got to advance her career. What a career, breaking her heart for tourists and niggers! She ought to go to Hollywood."

Blancanales took in the crowd around them.

"What's a Western saloon doing in Jamaica anyway?"

"It's a conspiracy. Prairie fairies of the world."

They laughed. Pardee raised his beer mug. "To you, Marchardo. And me. And all the soldiers like us. Right or wrong, we're real."

"There it is."

Pardee grinned. "And the marines!"

"What outfit were you in?" Blancanales asked.

"101st Airborne. Death From Above. Winged Victory." Pardee's grin suddenly became a sneer. "The PAVN couldn't stop us but a goddamned army of hippies and politicians did."

The backstage door opened again. A young blond woman in a black velvet pantsuit and ten-gallon hat carried a guitar to the stage. Pardee's sour look faded. He watched her admiringly as she adjusted the microphone, tuned her guitar. "God, she's so pretty," he said out loud.

While Pardee gazed at the girl on the stage, Blancanales studied Pardee. The man had a face scorched and creased by years of exposure. Squint lines marked the corners of his eyes. White sunburn scars splotched his high cheekbones. When Craig Pardee had sneered, Blancanales noticed a very limited mobility to the right side of his face. Now he saw why. A pattern of little scars crossed his face and disappeared into his short-cut hair.

Though Pardee stood six foot in street shoes, his muscles made him look squat. He wore a size nineteen collar. But despite his bulk, all his motions were fluid and precise. Pardee was a hard man. He was the image of the professional soldier.

Watching the girl now, however, he had the soft eyes and smile of a boy in love. Blancanales decided to drop it on Pardee:

"Oh, yeah. I want to introduce you to some friends of mine. They're good guys. And they're looking for work."

Pardee turned to Blancanales, his face suddenly expressionless, his eyes dead, but the arteries and tendons in his throat stood from his weathered skin.

"What?"

"Slow, Pardee. Slow. I didn't break your security. They don't know what's going on. They don't even know your name. I told them nothing. I just said there's a chance for work, and that I'd vouch for them. That's it. You say no, they fly on to Miami. No problem."

"Who are they?"

"We just came off a run. One guy's like me, a shooter. Great with a rifle, better with a pistol. The other guy's into electronics. Radio, radar, high-tech stuff. But when there's trouble, he knows how to rock and roll."

"Drugs?"

"It was work. There's no war on, so—"

"I mean them. They into drugs?"

"I've lived with them for weeks at a time, on ships, in neighborhoods. I never saw them do anything except a little alcohol. Pardee, you don't know that business. Dopers don't last long in the dope trade."

"What's their background?"

"Nam. Some police trouble. The shooter says he's on the run. The electronics man is clean."

"So what's he doing running dope?"

"Making money."

On the stage, the girl began her song. She accompanied herself with the guitar. Pardee turned away from Blancanales and watched her. He gently responded to the rhythm of the guitar chords as he sipped his beer, making it last. Blancanales waited.

The girl paused after her song and Pardee applauded. His clapping moved two or three other patrons to applaud. Blancanales joined in, but the applause was lost in the nonstop barroom noise. Pardee glared miserably at the tourists and phony cowfolk who were ignoring the girl. Then he demanded of Blancanales:

"Who else will recommend them?"

"Ask Señor Meza. Ask the people we both know. But I can't give you any other names—security works both ways. I didn't give anybody your name, I can't give anybody's name to you. They'd think you were Federal. And then it would be all over for me. But anybody on the yacht will vouch for them. They wiped out a hijack most professionally."

Without commenting, Pardee returned his attention to the girl. He listened to the several more songs in her set. He didn't ask any more questions of Blancanales.

The girl hit the last chords of her last song as the jukebox blasted away her final lyrics, drowning out the few patrons who had the courtesy to applaud.

She hurried off the stage and rushed through the backstage door.

"Assholes," Pardee muttered, casting a surly eye at the crowd. "Don't have good manners. They pay to hear a singer, then they don't listen. They work in an office, then dress up like cowboys. Civilians. I even see puke faggots wearing camouflage on the streets. Total mystery to me."

"They're bored," Blancanales replied. "They wear suits during the day, so they want something different. Like you, you're not in uniform. You're wearing a suit."

Pardee grinned. His smile looked like the fixed grimace of a skull. "Suit's just another uniform to me. You wouldn't believe how many suits I've ruined with other people's blood."

The girl arrived. "Craig, let's get out of here," she said immediately, pulling at Pardee's arm. She carried a guitar case and had an oversized purse over her shoulder, but no more Texas hat. She glanced at Blancanales. He saw tears streaming from her eyes.

Pardee threw money on the table, then followed the girl through the crowd. Blancanales followed Pardee.

Blancanales fell back for an instant and spoke to the miniature microphone in his lapel. "We're coming out."

Waiting in the parking lot, Gadgets and Lyons heard their partner's announcement through the earphones of the radio receiver. They slouched down in the rented car's seats.

At the exit, Pardee turned to Blancanales. "We'll

drop her off first. Then we'll go down to the docks.''

"My friends are outside in the—"

But Pardee didn't hear. He saw the club manager standing with a waitress. Pointing his index finger like a pistol, Pardee sneered into his face: "You cater to lowlife assholes!"

The manager tried to slap the finger aside. Pardee drove the finger powerfully into the manager's solar plexus. The manager collapsed gasping.

In the parking lot, the girl cried as she walked. "I'm never going to sing in a beer bar again. Never! It is just so humiliating, it's so—"

"You were good," Pardee consoled her. "I couldn't hear you most of the time, but you sounded good. You looked good—"

She wiped away her tears. "I know I'm good. I'm crying because they didn't pay attention. I thought working an international resort would be classy, but it was just a beer bar."

Four toughs in black shirts and pants, the uniform of the local gangs, lounged against a car. When they saw the three foreigners approaching, the gang boys stopped talking and stared. One tough put his hand under his shirt.

Pardee's right hand went toward his left underarm as he stepped toward the four youths. Then motion blurred on the near side of them. Blancanales lunged to grab that fifth punk, but it was too late. The girl shrieked.

The fifth punk jerked her head back by her hair, put an eight-inch blade to her throat. "Drop dat pistol, fat man!"

Pardee pointed a .45 Auto-Colt at the four gang boys. He turned, pointed the pistol at the fifth. The punk ducked behind the girl, shielding himself. He peeked out at Pardee as he pressed the knife against the girl's throat.

"Drop it or she die here!"

Thumbing down the hammer, Pardee glanced at Blancanales, then slowly stooped down and surrendered the Colt to the asphalt. One of the gang boys ran forward and kicked Pardee in the gut. Pardee did not even look at the gang boy. He kept his eyes on the punk with the knife.

Two toughs shoved Blancanales against a car and went through his pockets. The others slammed at Pardee with their fists, hitting him in the body, then in the face, their fists sounding like slaps. Still he kept his eyes on the punk with the knife.

Blancanales muttered into the tiny microphone set in his coat lapel. "Lyons, Gadgets. Trouble. Real trouble. Other side of the club."

"Shut that mouth, white man," a tough screamed at him. Blancanales blocked a punch with his elbow.

"Thanks for the money, man, thanks for the gun, and man, thanks for the blonde!" shrieked the punk who was pointing the surrendered .45 at Pardee's head. "You know what we gonna do? We all gonna screw her, then—"

The tough holding the knife to the girl's throat stepped close to Pardee, leered into his face:

"—we gonna take her across town and sell her—"

Pardee glanced at the .45 only a foot from his head. He smiled, looked over to Blancanales. Pol studied the pistol for an instant. The punk had thumbed its hammer back only to half-cock.

In a motion too fast to see, Pardee snatched the knife from the punk with the girl. The tough with the pistol jerked the trigger, but there was no shot. Pardee kicked and punched. Toughs slammed backward into cars. The auto-pistol clattered to the asphalt.

Blancanales smashed the hoodlums on either side of him, then sprinted for the girl. Even as he kicked the punk who had threatened the singer, the girl punched the punk in the throat, knocking him down and out. Blancanales pulled the enraged girl away.

Turning, Blancanales saw Pardee lean over the two thrashing, choking gang boys that he had kicked and punched. The choking ended in strange gaspings. When Pardee stood, his hands and coat sleeves were glistening with blood. The eight-inch blade of his knife dripped red.

"Down!" Carl Lyons shouted from the far end of the parking lot. "Get down!"

One of the toughs had a snub-nosed revolver. Blancanales shoved the girl down, threw himself on top of her.

The rip-roar of the Magnum's bullet passed over them. Blancanales heard glass falling as the bullet, punching through the toughboy, continued on through parked cars.

Pardee stooped down to Blancanales. "Get Christie out of here. We'll meet at the hotel. Go!"

"Craig—" the blond singer called out "—are you okay?"

"We're going to the car, come on." Blancanales jerked Christie to her feet, then half-dragged her across the parking lot.

Behind them popped six small-caliber shots. Blancanales saw Pardee empty the .22 snub-nose at the club's side exit. Someone ducked back inside and slammed the door closed. Pardee wiped the revolver of prints and dropped it. Then he cut the throats of the two toughs that Blancanales had sent sprawling against the car.

Carl Lyons caught Christie's arm, took her stubbornly held guitar case. "Are you hurt, lady?"

"I'm okay! Who are you?"

"He's a friend. We've got to get you out of here. Where's your car?" Blancanales' voice pulsed with urgency.

"We came in Craig's."

"Then we'll take mine. He'll follow us."

Blancanales had the doors to his rented sedan open in an instant. Lyons and Gadgets helped the singer into the car, then sprinted for their car.

A long scream tore apart the night. Blancanales looked back to the bodies. He saw Pardee, knife in one hand, something gory in the other, standing over the wailing, writhing punk who had threatened Christie. The scream choked off as Pardee jammed the handful of gore into the punk's mouth. Then he lifted the punk's head by the hair and grinned his death's-head smile into the face of the dying gang boy.

The knife flashed twice. Blood arced from the hood's yawning throat.

Blancanales threw the rented car into gear, burned rubber. A last look into the rearview mirror showed Pardee pause in the center of the parking lot to survey the scene, then scoop up his Colt from the asphalt and run to his car.

Taking directions from Christie, Blancanales wove through the avenues of Kingston. Lyons and Gadgets followed in their rented car. Pardee was waiting for them at the hotel. He greeted Lyons with a grin and a handshake.

"Good shooting, pal. Two inches to the left of the sternum at one hundred feet. And by street light. Ex-cell-ent!"

"Thanks. Practice makes perfect."

"Marchardo! You see the expression on that punk's face when he pulls the trigger and nothing? Punk didn't know the difference between cocked and half-cocked." Pardee continued on to Christie. "Are you all right, love?"

"I'm okay. What about you? You're the one they kicked."

"We don't have time to talk. My friend here—" he nodded to Lyons "—had to kill one of those punks. You know how the law is. I'm sending you back to the States. Or anywhere you want to go right now. We can't stay in Jamaica."

"I'll go with you. I don't want to go back alone."

"Okay, Los Angeles. You always wanted to go to L.A., so now you're going. Upstairs and pack! I'll join you in California next weekend."

Christie ran into the hotel. Pardee watched her, a look of love on his face. He turned to the three men.

"Okay, gentlemen. You got work." Pardee offered his hand to Gadgets. Then he noticed the blood that had clotted on his jacket sleeves. He grinned at Blancanales:

"Another good suit hits the shitcan."

5

Dawnlight revealed the desert blurring beneath them, rocks and low brush flashing past at three hundred miles per hour. The pilot maintained an altitude of one hundred feet. To the east, rip-saw peaks stood black against a horizon the color of sheet flame. Six hours out of Jamaica, this was their first sight of Texas. They had seen the distant glows of towns' lights during the night. But now, in the first minutes of daylight, there was nothing. They skimmed over total isolation. Only the black line of a highway miles off marked the desert.

"So—you worked for the airlines after your discharge..." Pardee continued his questioning. For the hours of the flight, the plush leather and hardwood interior of the Beechcraft jetprop had served as an interrogation room. Before take-off, Pardee had collected their weapons and searched them. In the air, he asked them for their backgrounds, in detail. And then he questioned each detail.

"For a while, yeah," Gadgets answered. "But they let me go. Either the Feds bothered them, or they decided not to risk me fragging a pilot. They never told me straight."

"If you fragged your captain in Nam, how come they hired you in the first place?"

The nature of his role damn near made Hermann Gadgets Schwarz spit.

"I didn't tell them. I had a medical discharge. I had my Purple Heart. I mean, it was 'Hire the Vet' time. Until the investigators came along. Then they found out."

"What was the name of your captain? The one you wasted."

"Sisson. Captain Sissy, I called him. Always having us running around topside, to string antennas and put up new radar dishes—but he wouldn't even go for his own food. One time we took a hit on top that took away our gear, and he orders three men up to fix it. To fix it right then. Rockets, mortars, 130mm shells coming down, and he sends them up. 'Wouldn't ask you to do anything I wouldn't do.' Bang, we get hit again. He sends me up to check on them. Nothing but rags and meat. Couldn't even tell who was who. I go down and give him the bad news, he hears it, then he sends me topside to the officers' mess. He has me fetch coffee. The sky's falling, we're dying all over, and I'm trying not to spill his coffee." Schwarz was alive to the possibilities of the story. In fact he knew many like it. "That's when I decided to do him. My contribution to the war effort."

"How'd you do it?" Pardee pressed.

The invention burned on. "Told a recon I knew that I wanted Chicom 82mm mortar. Then I put an electric Claymore's blasting cap on the fuse, and hid it just a little bit inside one of the sandbags topside. He went topside, I popped him, then I pulled the wires clear. I jammed them in my pocket as I went to help him. I tied off what was left of his legs and arm but he bled to death before he got to triage. His replacement had a more realistic attitude.''

"I was in Operation Pegasus," Pardee commented. "Never saw a more fucked-up place than Khe Sanh. When did you say you met Mr. Marchardo?''

Blancanales interrupted. "Pardee, can't you lighten up? Luther and I go back years and years."

Luther. Luther Schwarz.

"Gentlemen," Pardee told them, looking at each of them. He smiled his death's-head grin. "You answer all the questions I ask you. Or you take a walk. Do we understand each other?''

"No problem here," Lyons told him.

"Thank you, Mr. Morgan."

Carl Morgan.

Outside, the jagged spines of mountains towered on both sides. Air turbulence shook the Beechcraft.

"When did you meet Mr. Marchardo?''—

Gadgets looked to Blancanales. "When was it? A couple of years ago. The time the coast guard played tracer-tag with that yacht full of hippie dopers...."

"Oh, man...." Blancanales laughed.

"Were you there, Mr. Morgan?''

"No."

"How long have *you* worked with your friends?''

"This year."

"Tell me all about it."

"Sometimes we're on boats. Sometimes we fly. Sometimes I get a G-3. Sometimes it's a Mattie Mattel. Always I got my Python. What else you interested in?''

"Who you really are."

Lyons didn't answer for a second. Gadgets looked out the window, watched the morning sun light the rocks. If Lyons couldn't handle this questioning. . . .

"I'm past that." Lyons spoke like an old man.

"What?" Pardee looked piercingly at Lyons. "Just give me a straight answer."

"I'm Carl Morgan. I've got a phony passport and a Colt Python with a magnaported six-inch barrel. Issue me a rifle, I'll carry it. What else can I tell you?"

"You and me just might get along, Morgan," Pardee said. "Last night, I asked your pal for references. He said he couldn't talk about it. But you two will. I want the names of people you worked for. You're on the payroll, but until I check you out, you don't get weapons, briefings, nothing. Understand?"

"No problem here," Lyons told him.

"I understand," Gadgets agreed.

The intercom interrupted them. "One minute until landing. One minute."

The three men of Able Team looked out as the base flashed beneath them. They saw rows of steel prefab buildings, asphalt streets, gravel assembly areas, and a two-lane highway. The highway cut through the rocky hills around the camp, continued past the camp to a mansion set on the peak of a distant hill. Two fences surrounded the base. A blockhouse guarded the only gate.

"There is something you should know," Pardee

cut off their sight-seeing. "Texas has a whole different attitude about private property. Somebody
goes someplace, and they ain't supposed to be there,
that's trespassing. And like the sign on the fence
down there says, 'Trespassers Will Be Shot.'"

The Beechcraft's wheels touched the landing strip.

Below his office window in La Paz, waves of flowers
rolled across the red clay tiles of the restaurant roof.
Parrots squawked on the patio. The flowers attracted
hummingbirds.

Bob Paxton turned from his desk to watch the
emerald-green birds flit through the flowers. Once,
when ravens had raided the nests of the tiny birds,
eating the eggs and chicks, Paxton had taken his silenced Ruger .22 and dropped the ravens, one by one.

Now he held the Ruger under his desk. The footsteps on the creaky stairs continued to his door.
Before the visitor knocked, Paxton crossed the office, his feet silent on the tiles except for the slight
squeak of the ankle on his plastic leg.

Knock. "Señor Paxton, this is Lieutenant Navarro."

Paxton slipped the Ruger in his belt at the small of
his back. He opened the door for the young lieutenant. The two men presented a contrast in military
traditions: Paxton, the ex-gunnery sergeant with his
beer belly and cocaine habit; Navarro, slim and for-
mal in his tailored polyester. Yet Navarro respected
the boozy retired non-com. Unlike Navarro, Paxton
had distinguished himself in combat. Navarro knew
he would never have the opportunity.

"How can I help you, Lieutenant?"

The young Latin handed him a folder. Paxton glanced through the eight-by-ten black-and-white blow-ups.

"I need to know the names and nationalities."

"I don't know about these three, I'll have to check my files," said Paxton. "But this man—" He limped to his desk, spread out the photos. "I can tell you who he is, right now."

Paxton put his finger on the glossy black-and-white photo of Hal Brognola.

6

A closed van waited only steps from the jetprop.
Scanning the scene as they left the plane, they saw the
concrete landing strip, strips of landing lights, the
steel prefab hangars at the far end. Double chain link
fences topped with razor wire encircled the area.

"Move it!" Pardee shouted. "No tourism! In the
truck."

Sitting on the floor of the van, Blancanales felt the
air compress as Pardee slammed the van doors shut
on them. "Reminds me of prison."

Gadgets touched his ear, pointed to the walls of the
van. Blancanales and Lyons nodded. "Way I see it,"
Gadgets said clearly, "they run a tight operation.
And I'm glad. Most of the gangs down South don't
get busted from the outside, it's always a Fed or an
informer on the inside. So a tight operation is all
right with me."

The van took them first to an infirmary. Again, in
the few steps between the van and the door of the
prefab infirmary, they saw almost nothing of the
base: chain link fencing topped by razor wire, and a
blacktop road.

"Strip down," an orderly told them. He gave them
each a deep plastic tray. "All your clothes and per-

sonal things in the trays. And I mean everything. Rings, dogtags, all of it.''

"When do we get it back?" Lyons asked. "And where's our luggage?"

"Hey, man," the bone-thin blond orderly drawled in his southern accent. "Until you clear Security, that's the least of your worries."

Naked, they waited until a doctor took them one by one into an examination room. A middle-aged man with the gray skin and ravaged body of an alcoholic, the doctor did not introduce himself nor question them on their medical histories. Speaking only in monosyllables, he took full-body photographs of them, complete X rays, then blood samples.

Next, the orderly gave them each day-glow orange fatigues and tennis shoes, and hurried them back to the van.

"Dig these jazzy uniforms," Gadgets sighed.

"Camouflage," Lyons said. "For an invasion of Las Vegas."

Another short ride and the van dropped them at their barrack. The building sat at the edge of the base. It looked like a prison unit. Two electric gates and a glass-walled guard booth completed the impression created by the chain link fence and razor wire.

A man standing six-foot-eight stomped from the barrack door. "Stop rubbernecking, new meat. In here!"

They filed through. The interior was one large room. Two rows of ten steel bunk beds ran the length

of the barrack. Though there were scuffs in the
linoleum and chips in the paint of the steel beds, the
place had the smell of a new house trailer, just
months old. The sheet steel walls had the original
enamel. Not one of the windows was cracked.

"I am Sergeant Cooke," the three-hundred-pound
soldier told them. "Until Captain Pardee is positive
on your identities, you stay here. When you clear
Security, you will join the other men. Until then, you
sweat. Here are the supplies you need for the next
few days."

He pointed to a table. There were three identical
piles of sheets, pillowcases, blankets, soaps, razors.

"I suggest you make your bunks now. Tonight you
might not have it left in you." Sergeant Cooke threw
back his immense shoulders, glared at each of them
for an instant, and added: "I'm taking you out for a
long walk."

Ten miles into the rocky foothills, Sergeant Cooke
collapsed. He floundered in the dust, trying to stand,
but got no further than his hands and knees. He fell
onto his back, gasping, his face gray and streaming
with sweat.

Blancanales sat at the side of the trail, watching
Sergeant Cooke struggle. Gadgets looked down at
the huge man. Lyons squinted into the afternoon
glare. He shaded his eyes and scanned the horizon.

"You think they're training over there?" Lyons
pointed to the east. "Every once in a while, I hear
booms. Thought I saw a helicopter."

"Take a break, Morgan," Blancanales told him.

"We got a problem here with the D.I. Looks like heatstroke to me."

"Textbook case," Gadgets agreed.

"What's with you guys?" Sergeant Cooke croaked. "Pardee hire you straight out of the Special Forces?"

Gadgets flashed a grin to Blancanales and Lyons. "Sort of."

The second day, Sergeant Cooke rode a 1200cc dirt bike while Able Team double-timed.

High above the rocks and red dust of the Texas desert, Tate Monroe surveyed the maneuvers of his mercenary army from the helicopter of its commander, Colonel Furst. Monroe leaned against the nylon safety webbing to peer down at the other helicopters circling beneath them. In the brilliant sunlight, his hair looked like strands of ceramic, the skin of his tropics-scarred face like translucent plastic molded over a skull. He wore antique sunglasses, round black lenses on a wire frame. The round lenses looked like black eye sockets.

"There's the objective," Colonel Furst shouted over the rotor noise. Furst was square-shouldered, with muscles straining his tailored fatigues. Years of combat and prison had not marred his movie-star good looks.

Furst pointed to a series of concrete buildings alongside an asphalt road. The buildings had only walls and roofs. Along the road, several old cars and trucks were parked.

"Here comes the lead ship now," Furst shouted. "Inside that helicopter, there's a hundred steel tubes, all loaded with 106mm recoilless rifle rounds and triggered electrically. It's very effective. Watch.''

Dropping down, a Huey paralleled the road at a hundred miles an hour. An instant before it came to the buildings and the parked vehicles, the Huey climbed suddenly, then banked. Fire flashed from its side.

A chain of explosions ripped the road and clustered buildings. Blazing seconds later, gutted hulks burned on the road. Dust and billowing smoke obscured the buildings. Wheeling in the sky, the Huey swept down again. A second chain of explosions hit the buildings and vehicles from the opposite direction. Shattered concrete and twisted metal was all that remained.

''That was twenty rounds,'' Furst announced, ''leaving eighty rounds in reserve. Now here's the clean-up squad. The other troops take blocking positions.''

Three Hueys swept in low, the door gunners spraying the target with machine-gun fire. One touched down near the wrecked trucks. The second and third split, the second landing on the road three hundred yards to the north, the third three hundred yards to the south. The squad from the first helicopter sprinted into the smoke and fire. The other two squads fanned out along the road.

''The clean-up squad makes sure that everything is dead,'' Colonel Furst concluded.

''Excellent,'' Monroe nodded, leaning back against the seat. He rested his head against the bulkhead and mouthed the word again. "Excellent. Excellent."

Electronic funk filled the interior of the limousine. Half-smiling, her face a mask of Quaalude pleasure, Mrs. Monroe swayed slightly to the rhythm. Her features revealed her heritage, her defined, almost aquiline nose and high cheekbones showing her Indian blood, her full lips and round eyes the Spanish. Designer clothes and gold jewelry revealed her wealth.

Dr. Nathan, Tate Monroe's personal physician, glanced into the searing blue of the midday sky. A thin, pale young man from New York City, he sucked hard on the last inch of a cigarette, opened the limo door for an instant to flick the butt outside. Then he lit another with the limo's gold lighter.

"Mrs. Monroe, this is absurd. Your husband contracted me as his doctor. I have no responsibilities other than his health. I cannot—by contract—ever be more than one minute away. I am on call twenty-four hours a day. Which is all very reasonable, considering the condition of his heart.

"But what does he do? He goes up in a helicopter. What does he say to me? 'Wait here, I'll be back in an hour.' Do you have any idea what kind of stress that will put on his heart? I don't mean just the excitement of flying around in the sky with his security personnel, I mean the altitude!

"The higher someone goes, Mrs. Monroe, the more demand on that muscle, and your husband has

one sick muscle in his chest. I cannot believe what
he—''

"Only another month, doctor," Mrs. Monroe interrupted. She turned to him, her eyes heavy-lidded
with drugs. "Perhaps sooner. Can you not have pa-
tience with...your patient—" She laughed at her
pun, throwing her head back against the seat, and the
laugh died. She closed her eyes, rubbed her cheek
against the leather of the seat. "Only another
month," she murmured.

"Mrs. Monroe," Dr. Nathan began.

"Please call me Availa. I tell you so often—"

"Mrs. Monroe. Your husband may not survive the
year if he continues disregarding my instructions. I
don't want to have—"

Availa Monroe came upright, her eyes suddenly
hard, her lips curling in disdain. "You don't want!
What does it matter what you want? If my husband—" she spat the word "—has another month of
life, he will have his revenge. And that is all he wants.
What you want, what I want, it is nothing. Want...."

Her anger gone, she lay back against the seat
again, her eyes closing. She spoke without opening
her eyes. "Tell me, doctor. What is my age?"

Dr. Nathan studied her face with concern. "Those
pills are dangerous. They are habit-forming and have
long-term toxic effects—"

"My age, doctor."

"Twenty-five and months."

She laughed. "Thank you for lying, doctor. But I
know I am so very old. I have so much to forget. I
must be old."

"Mrs. Monroe—Availa, please. I don't know your troubles, not all of them, but if you want help—counseling, medication, or just someone to talk to you—you're a very rich woman. You don't need to suffer in silence, you don't need to drug yourself so...."

Dr. Nathan reached out to her.

She jerked her hand away, hissing. "Don't touch me!"

They heard the throb of approaching helicopters. Dr. Nathan lit another cigarette from the butt of the one he smoked, and stepped into the hot desert wind.

In the red glow of sunset, Able Team jogged back to the base. Salt crusted in sweat patterns on their orange jumpsuits. Sergeant Cooke roared past them on his dirt bike, his wheels throwing dust and gravel into the air. Running blind through the dust, Gadgets tripped on a rock and fell.

Lyons helped him up. "That Cooke irritates me."

"Yeah." Gadgets wiped blood from his torn hands. "I think he's doing it deliberately."

"Lots of deliberate things can happen to him, too." Lyons ran alongside Gadgets. "But that has to wait."

"But how much longer?" Gadgets gasped. "This waiting is about to kill me. We must've done a hundred miles today."

Lyons laughed. "It's good for you."

"Ughhhhhhh," Gadgets groaned.

Ahead of them, where the trail met the asphalt

road, they saw a jeep. The two previous evenings, after their forced marches through the desert and hills, it had been the closed van that had taken them into the base. Now they saw Blancanales swing into the jeep.

Lyons sprinted to the road. "All right! Did we finally get our clearance?"

"Sure did, pal," the driver told him. A crew-cut, muscled man with a black mustache, the driver extended a strong hand to Lyons. "I'm Perkins. Welcome to the Texas Irregulars."

Cold wind from the Andes banged signs, carried newspapers down the avenue. The wind penetrated the old weather-stripping of his Volkswagen's doors, chilled Bob Paxton's stump despite the heater. He massaged the ache where his right leg ended, not bothering to downshift until he came to El Negro's villa. Then he threw the shift into first, and chugged up to the iron gate.

Paxton kept his hands on the wheel as the guards approached. There was one man on each side, both with folding stock Galil assault rifles. Then a third man shone a flashlight in Paxton's face. He waved the light over the interior of the small car. He signaled the guard window. An electric motor opened the heavy gates.

Ex-Lieutenant Navarro approached as Paxton parked in front of the villa. "Señor Paxton, do you have everything?"

"Most everything." Carrying a folder of photos and papers, Paxton limped after the young man into the villa. Hardfaced men with Uzi's and sawed-off shotguns watched them from the shadows.

The warmth of the foyer washed over Paxton, relaxing him, easing the ache where his leg had been. They paused while a guard went over Paxton with a hand-held metal detector, then they continued to the library. Navarro opened the door for him.

"It is my pleasure to introduce Master Sergeant Robert Paxton, Retired." Navarro announced.

El Negro stood to greet the American. Unusually tall for a Bolivian, almost six feet, the man had coarse features and blue black hair, swept straight back from his forehead. He shook Paxton's hand. "My aide tells me you have important information for me."

"Information, yes. But I hope it is of no importance to you." Paxton spread photos across El Negro's walnut desk. "Lieutenant Navarro brought these photos to me. He believed them to be either a new American gang in Bolivia or new Drug Enforcement Agency officers. Three men I can't identify, yet. But this man is well known in the United States.

"He is Hal Brognola, formerly of the United States Department of Justice. Specializing in organized crime until last year. What he's doing now is unknown—"

"Organized crime?" El Negro asked.

"The big gangs in North America and Europe. The Mafia, the Syndicate. Anyone who has the smarts to get organized. But most of that is over now. In the last year of Mr. Brognola's service, the gangs took heavy, heavy casualties. Most of the gangs were wiped out.''

"And the other three men?"

"Nothing on them. Zero."

"Lieutenant Navarro, you will work with Mr. Paxton. Whatever it costs, wherever you must go. I want to know why they are in my country. It is, Mr. Paxton, very important to me."

7

Dust whirled in the wind. Twisting into a red column, the swirl obscured the sun, throwing the firing range in shadow. The paper targets at fifty feet, one hundred feet, and three hundred feet flapped as the dust devil swept past. Then the wind shifted, and the whirling column lost its vortex, became a cloud of churning, billowing grit.

Pardee pulled a bandanna up over his mouth and nose. Like his uniform, the bandanna was khaki splotched with gray and rust—the colors of desert camouflage. Now Blancanales, Gadgets, and Lyons wore the uniforms of the mercenary army also.

"I saw what you could do the other night," Pardee told Lyons. "But that was your pistol. And maybe you're lucky with your own weapon. Give me the same show with this M-16."

Taking the loaded rifle, Lyons pulled out the magazine, snapped back the action to check the chamber, then hinged open the receiver. He glanced at the interior, then closed the rifle. He sat down at a shooting bench, resting the rifle on a table.

"Hey, no bench-resting it," Pardee told him. "Stand up and rapid fire."

"I'll zero it first."

"It's good, I zeroed it myself."

"No one prepares my weapon but me," Lyons told him. "It's a habit that's kept me alive."

"Go ahead, Morgan. Be difficult."

Sighting on the fifty-foot target, Lyons punched a 5.56mm hole through the printer's seal in the lower left hand corner. He stood, snapping the stock to his shoulder, fired three rounds, shifted his aim, fired three more rounds, then aimed at the 300-foot target, fired three times again.

Focusing his binoculars, Pardee counted the hits. "Three tens on the fifty, two...three in the black of the hundred-foot target. And on the hundred yard...two in the black."

Blancanales laughed, gave Lyons a shove. "Slipping up, hotshot."

"Morgan" shrugged. "It's windy." He pulled out the magazine, jerked back the action to clear the chamber. He caught the flying cartridge, and handed the rifle to Blancanales.

"Wait a second, Marchardo." Pardee pointed to Lyons' personal weapon, the Colt Python that he wore in a shoulder holster. "Now your wheel-gun, two bullets each target."

In one fluid motion, Lyons swept the Python from his holster as he dropped into a wide-legged stance. He fired six times in six seconds.

"The ten's gone on the fifty, you got three in the black of the hundred, and two blacks on the hundred-yard target." Pardee lowered the binoculars. "You are a shooter."

Lyons ejected the Magnum's brass into his hand. He pocketed the casings. "I work at it."

"Wish we had time." Pardee glanced downrange at the targets. "I'd put you to work as an instructor. Some of our quote soldiers unquote need a full mag to put a scare on a target. Now you, Marchardo. Semi-auto rapid fire."

Blancanales fired twice at the fifty-foot target, and raised the rifle to sight on the hundred-foot target. Pardee stopped him:

"Back to the fifty-foot target, blindman. Fire until you hit it."

"I got two tens. Morgan ripped up the bull's-eye with his cannon. My rounds went through the holes."

"Quit the talk. Put some holes on that paper."

"Two tens so far." Blancanales snapped the rifle to his shoulder, called his shots. "Number nine to the right, eight to the right, seven."

Downrange, 5.56 holes stitched across the paper target, punching out the numbers 9 and 8 and 7 in the score rings.

"All right, Marchardo." Pardee grinned. "Big shot. Now give me a good pattern on the hundred-yard target."

Brass arced through the air as Blancanales fired, the shots one roar of sound. The bolt locked back after the last cartridge. Blancanales pulled out the magazine and blew smoke from the receiver like a space-age gunfighter.

"You pass. Now Luther." Pardee tossed a magazine to Gadgets.

"I have to shoot those torn-up targets? How will you know what I score?"

"Then put up some new ones. There's the targets, there's the staple gun, go to it."

"Forget the walking," Gadgets muttered. "Numero cinco, to the left." He fired three times. "Same thing on the hundred." He fired again, then sighted on the hundred-yard target, punched holes in the black. "Good enough?"

"All of you are very good." Pardee took up the M-16. He cleared the chamber.

"What's with using M-16s, Pardee?" Blancanales asked. "And these desert uniforms. From what I see in newspapers and magazines, we'll look like Rapid Deployment troopers. Someone could get the idea we're official."

"That's not my worry," Pardee replied. "What I need is shooters. But what I got is full-auto noise-makers."

"Put them out here on the range," Lyons suggested. "Can't you afford the ammo?"

Pardee shook his head. "Can't afford the time. Chances are, in two weeks all of this will be history."

On the wide-screen television screen, a helicopter closed on a cluster of concrete buildings and parked cars and trucks. Fire streaked from the side of the helicopter, blast-flashes and clouds of flame obscured the targets.

Another video clip showed desert-camouflaged soldiers crowded into a helicopter. The image jumped and wavered with the bucking of the helicopter as the ground rushed up to meet the camera. The camera lurched, soldiers jumped from the side door, sprinted into flames and drifting black smoke.

The sound track carried rotor-throb, shouted commands, staccato auto-rifle bursts.

In a final clip, the cameraman leaned from the side door of his helicopter to pan over the blocking forces in positions around the road. As he passed the squad, his camera recorded the blasted buildings and wrecks, soldiers moving through the smoke and debris, then showed the second blocking force.

"Attack, deployment, and withdrawal in five minutes," Colonel Furst told the others as he switched off the video deck and switched on the lights. He turned to them, his boots shoulder-width apart, his fists on his hips. He scanned their faces—the smiling Tate Monroe in his wheelchair, Craig Pardee in his dusty fatigues at Monroe's side, and Jorge Lopez in his five-hundred-dollar silk suit.

They sat in Monroe's trophy room. Photos of Monroe in his youth, mementos from his distant and now lost operations, and portraits of his past wives covered the walls. There was a wooden propeller. There were rifles, submachine guns, a Browning .50-caliber machine gun with the stenciled words, Monroe International, along its water-cooled barrel.

The back wall had ports for the projection room. In the past, Tate Monroe had entertained old friends with black-and-white movies of his adventures in the thirties, forties, and fifties. But he had outlived his friends. For the past several weeks, he had watched videotapes of preparations for another adventure, one which he had financed, but which would be the glory of other, younger men.

"What is your reaction, Señor Lopez?" Furst demanded of the elegant Mexican.

Lopez glanced at a notepad before answering. "His rancho is beyond the range of your helicopters."

"We will secure a staging area in your country before we make our strike."

"And where will that be?" Lopez asked.

Furst did not answer.

Lopez nodded, glanced at his notes again. "He is not without protection there. What if the helicopter with the rockets is shot down? What if one of your troop helicopters is shot down? Will you be able to complete your mission?"

"Affirmative. We have backup units. But we do not believe his security personnel will have the time to react. We will come in at one hundred feet, the lead helicopter will rocket all opposition, all buildings, all vehicles. I believe our greatest difficulty will be in finding the body. If we were willing to risk a one-percent chance of failure, we would have modified all the helicopters to fire rockets. Then we would have blasted the entire ranch flat and hoped we got him. But instead, we will take the time to find the body. There may be skirmishing and casualties, but we will be one hundred percent sure he is dead."

"Very good, Colonel Furst," Monroe said, his voice a rattle of mucous. He turned to Señor Lopez. "I have reviewed all of the colonel's plans. He has anticipated every contingency. He has recruited the finest independent soldiers and technicians and officers available. Every man has had months of training. Every man knows that success means wealth—not just generous pay, but lifelong wealth. Some of them may die, but those who live will be paid immediately what common men earn in a lifetime." The old man cleared his throat. "Tell all of this to your leader. We have already joined our families, soon we will join our destinies. We wait only for your signal."

"Yes, destiny..." muttered Lopez, studying his notes. "How is the señora? Happy? Even when she was a child, in her father's mansion, on his estates, she did not have the wealth that she knows now."

Monroe smiled. "Availa is a joy to me every moment of my day. Her joy is my joy."

"Her brother misses her," Lopez informed him. "They were always together, you realize. But so it must be.... They had a blessed childhood, but she could not be a child forever. She needed a husband to make her complete, to make her a woman."

"What will you tell your Rojo?" Furst demanded, cutting into the Mexican's personal speech.

"I will tell my leader that our American friends have assembled the men and machines required to strike the first blow of our revolution. I will tell him that this army, commanded by his own brother-in-law, the honorable Mr. Monroe, will join the phalanx of warriors and leaders marching against the international communist conspiracy. Together we will wield the swords of patriotism, liberty, and faith. We will—"

Furst's snickering interrupted Lopez. Pardee burst into guffaws. Offended, Lopez looked from one man to the other, and his face went taut with anger. Monroe stopped the laughter with a slap on the arm-rest of his invalid chair.

"Wheel me out," Monroe ordered Pardee. "Señor Lopez, dinner and my lovely wife wait for us. These soldiers wish to return to their troops. They have no time for talk. Or for cultured conversation."

"They have time for this much more talk." Lopez faced the soldiers and spoke with fierce anger. "Your films are very impressive, but they mean nothing. Your plans mean nothing. The battle alone will prove your worth. You talk brave now, you promise us his death. But until he is dead, you and your soldiers are the greatest threat facing our patriots. Your attack must be perfect. Perfect! If you fail, if you blunder, the Mexican government will believe that the United States government sponsored the attack, and there will be war. Not war between our patriots and the Marxists—but total, tragic war between our two nations!"

For a moment there was silence. Furst and Pardee did not dare mock the Mexican's statement. Then from an old, dried throat came the words that hissed through the withered, colorless lips of Tate Monroe:

"So be it!"

Their fatigues snapped in the warm dusk wind. Craig Pardee was letting gravity pull the open jeep through the curves and straightaways of the hills below Monroe's mansion. He gulped from a bottle of fine French wine he had stolen from the mansion's wine rack, passed it to Colonel Furst. Furst finished the bottle in two gulps. He heaved it into the canyon below the road. Arcing over the gathering shadows, the bottle flashed with the sunset's red light, then smashed on the stark eroded rocks.

Furst grinned, showing his movie-star teeth. "All Monroe wants is dead Mexicans. All the political talk, all that patriotism stuff, he don't care. . . ."

"I thought he wanted his oil fields back," Pardee said to his commander, "the ones he had way back when. The ones that got nationalized."

"He wants the fields because the Mexicans took them. When we first sketched out the plan, he had me look into getting a hydrogen bomb so that—"

"What?"

"An H-bomb. A super-nuke. He wanted to drop it on the oil fields. I figured I'd have to hijack three B-52s from the Strategic Air Command to do it right. So he decided to finance the revolution instead. I tell you, that old man has money. He had me running all over the world with suitcases full of hundred-dollar bills. Lear jets. Gold bullion." Furst grinned to Pardee. "You know how much the señorita cost?"

"I thought she was part of the political deal."

"At any price. And I think she has an erotic fascination with wheelchairs."

They laughed for a minute. Pardee pulled another bottle of wine from under the seat. They were parallel to the airfield now; miles away, the lights of the mercenary base sparkled in the twilight. Furst took the bottle, flicked out his German paratrooper knife, got the cork out.

"No time to waste," Furst joked. "Officers can't drink in front of the enlisted men. So, she is part of the politics, the señora is. And ten million dollars was part of the politics, too. Ever seen ten million in small bills?"

"Why didn't you just take off? Make for the horizon!"

Furst gave Pardee a knowing grin. "Then Monroe would send *you* after me. And if I offed you, he'd send ten more. And if I got them, he'd send a hundred. You don't mess with someone who can buy every freelance shooter in the world. Makes for bad experiences."

"Speaking of shooters, I got three new recruits who're good. One man's great."

"You still hiring men? We don't have time to train them."

"They don't need it. They're trainer material themselves. One guy speaks Mexican, one guy's a deadeye, pistols and rifles, and one's supposed to be an electronics freak. I'm going to work them into the raid tomorrow night."

"An electronics man?" Furst wondered out loud. "And a marksman? Let's talk to these fellows."

The base offered two first-run movies a night. Walking to the theater next to the PX, Lyons and Blancanales saw a jeep driven by Craig Pardee stop at the gate. The sentries saluted the two men in the open jeep, and the electric gates started open.

"I wonder who the hardcase with Pardee is," Blancanales said to Lyons. There was no answer. Blancanales glanced around for his friend. He was alone in the roadway.

"Hsst!" The signal came from the shadows between the prefab offices.

"What's with you, Morgan?" Blancanales stepped into the darkness. "What—"

Even in the shadows, Blancanales saw the panic in Lyons' eyes. Blancanales pushed Lyons farther back into total darkness.

"What's wrong?" Blancanales whispered.

Lyons forced his voice to be calm. "I want you to denounce me. Tell Pardee I said something, I did something. Tell him I wanted you to get a message out to the Feds. Anything."

"What're you talking about? They'll take you apart, you'll die."

"Do it fast and you can save yourself and Gadgets. The officer next to Pardee, that's Robert Furst. Last time I saw him was in court. I helped put him away for five years, armed robbery. I tell you, I'm dead."

8

Mercenaries stood to attention as Furst and Pardee strode into the barracks. Men abandoned magazines and checkerboards, stood beside their bunks. Wearing towels, pressed fatigues, or embroidered Afghan smoking robes, they saluted as their officers passed.

"Luther Schwarz!" Pardee shouted.

Sprawled on his upper bunk, Gadgets looked toward the loud voice as his hand went to the razor-sharp bayonet under his pillow. But he noted that Pardee and the other officer had no armed soldiers with them. Gadgets slid off the bunk and saluted.

"This is Commander Furst," Pardee announced. "I told him you are an electronics technician. What is your specialty?"

"Tricks."

"What kind of tricks?" Pardee demanded.

"Electronic tricks."

"That doesn't tell us much," Furst broke in. "How about giving us a briefing on what you've done for other people?"

Gadgets glanced around to the crowd of mercenaries in the barrack room. He nodded toward the door. "Let's talk out there."

On the way out, they met Blancanales. "And

here's the man who speaks Mexican," Pardee told Furst.

"Join us," Furst said to Blancanales. "We might have an op for you tomorrow night."

Outside, Pardee leaned against the jeep. "So what can you do for us?"

"You said there's going to be an operation," Gadgets started. "Give me an idea of what your operation is, and I'll tell you how I can help."

"Where's Morgan?" Pardee asked Blancanales.

"He went to the movies. You need him?"

Pardee looked to Furst. Furst said, "I'll talk to him later. Here's what we're doing tomorrow night. At sunset, Captain Pardee is taking four troopships south. There's a doper base in the mountains down there. It has an airfield, thousands of gallons of fuel in tanks, good buildings, a defensible road. We need to take it intact. We need to take it quickly, so quickly that they can't get a message out on their radio. If your friend Morgan is familiar with a Starlite scope, we can use him. And you, Marchardo, we can use you and your Spanish. But I'm not sure how electronics could play a role."

"You're going south," Gadgets said. "Then the helicopters come back?"

Furst nodded.

"That means you'll be flying through American radar twice. Means you'll be in Mexico all night. That's two air forces that'll be looking to give you trouble. If you're flying treetop low, maybe they won't spot you. But what happens if they've got a plane with downward-looking radar? What if a dope patrol locks on you? You're going to have to get back here without it following you. And what happens if your doper target has radar? They can afford it.''

"We plan to drop the men on the far side of mountain," Furst told him. "Then march over the top.''

"Okay, but you can't have your soldiers walk all the way back here. So I could put together an assortment of anti-radar devices—I can't make the Hueys disappear, but I can confuse anyone who's chasing you.''

"With what?''

"You have an electronics shop here, for your radios and things,'' Gadgets said. Furst nodded. "Then take me there. I'll see what I can put together.''

Furst turned to Pardee. "Get a Starlite rifle from the armory, take Morgan out to the firing range, see how he does. I'll walk this man over to the electronics shop.''

"Come on, Marchardo,'' Pardee ordered Blancanales as he climbed into the jeep. "Looks like Morgan misses the movie.''

Staring at the screen without seeing the images, Lyons waited. The film's story followed the recruitment of a mercenary force to attack an African nation. After corporate executives struck an agreeable deal with the nation's leaders, the executives abandoned the soldiers of fortune to the mercy of thousands of Cuban-led Simba cutthroats. The scenes of death, dismemberment and heroism brought bursts of laughter from the real-life mercenaries in the audience. Soldiers guzzled their rations of beer, then threw the cans at the screen. Storms of popcorn flew in the air. Soldiers ad-libbed, shouting advice to the actors. Other soldiers argued with the advice.

Chaos and noise, so no one noticed Blancanales slip into the seat beside Lyons. "How's the flick?"

"No one's started shooting yet," Lyons replied.

Bursts of machine-gun fire, mortar blasts and screaming came from the screen. Blancanales pointed. "Then what's that?"

"I mean in here." Lyons indicated the audience of mercenaries around them. Both of them laughed briefly. Lyons asked: "What's going on?"

"Your shooting impressed Pardee, so you've got a chance. They want you and me to go on an operation tomorrow night. Furst went over to the electronics shop to see what Gadgets can do. Pardee's waiting outside. We're supposed to go out to the firing range and check you out on a Starlite. You sure Furst would recognize you?"

Lyons grinned. "You bet your life. And Gadgets' life too."

"Furst won't be out at the firing range. I think we should risk it, it'll be dark soon. You got a chance."

"What about tomorrow?"

"Tomorrow's another day."

They left the seats and wove through the shouting, beer-drinking, popcorn-heaving mercenaries. At the exit, Lyons stopped Blancanales:

"The way we have our stories worked out, I'm the

newcomer. You and Gadgets can deny it all. Turn me in, and you've got a chance."

Blancanales shook his head, no.

Searching through racks of components, Gadgets made a list. A plastic bucket containing discarded solid-state circuit boards toppled from the top of the rack and crashed to the floor. Gadgets glanced at the spilled circuit boards. He picked one up and scratched a component from the list.

Televisions filled the workshop. Remote-controlled pan/tilt/zoom units lined one wall. A technician cleaned a mass of gears with a fine brush as he talked with Furst:

"It's the sand. We can't keep it out of the housings. We have two or three units a day go down. And then we get sun-flares burned into the videcon tubes. We put on filters, we can't use the cameras at night. Without the filters, the cameras burn. I tell you, Texas is a rough place for this equipment—"

Furst ignored the technician. He called out to Gadgets: "You find what you need?"

Gadgets left the racks. "Here's what I can do for you."

Scanning the darkness of the firing range and the rocky foothills beyond, all of it green through the optics of the Starlite scope, Lyons found the bottles. He paused to fix each in the cross hairs, then popped each with a single round from the M-16.

"That's six," Pardee told him.

"Just a second...." Lyons saw a shape scurry

through the rocks. He waited. When it moved again, he fired.

"What was that?" Blancanales asked.

"A rat."

"A head shot, I suppose," Pardee joked.

"Nah, nothing fancy," Lyons replied. "I shot him through the heart."

"Okay, you're going south. Rest your feet tomorrow. In twenty-four hours, you got a twenty-mile hike, then target practice on Mexican dopers."

Slipping out the magazine and clearing the chamber, Lyons handed the rifle to Pardee. "I don't want to knock the equipment, but how about getting that scope on an M-14? Mattel's swell, but...."

"Heavy rifle. You willing to carry it?"

"Dopers need the heavy stuff. Might not notice a five-five-six."

Pardee laughed and slapped Lyons on the back. "That's the attitude! You have to meet Colonel Furst, he'd like you."

Headlights flashed on the road from camp. In the quiet of the rolling desert, the whine of an engine came to them.

"Well, there, Morgan. Looks like you meet the man immediately. Here." Pardee returned the M-16 to Lyons. "I think you'll be doing some more shooting."

As Pardee walked downslope to the parking area, Lyons snapped the magazine into the receiver and eased back the action to chamber a round. He looked at Blancanales and muttered:

"Maybe so."

Schwarz rode in the passenger seat. Despite the darkness and the slipwind of the open jeep, Gadgets was sketching a design in a notebook. He finished a detail, held the drawing up for Furst as he drove, a shaky flashlight beaming onto the drawing.

"That's what it would look like," Gadgets told him. "I can put that together from the materials in the shop."

On the range, Lyons looked down to the jeep, gripped the top-heavy M-16. Blancanales stepped close to him:

"We'll wait for him up here. If he recognizes—"

"*When* he recognizes me."

"Okay, when he recognizes you—"

"Bang, bang."

In the jeep, a beeping cut off Gadget's tech talk. Furst touched a pager on his belt. He braked as he pulled up to Pardee and the other jeep.

"Urgent call," Furst told Pardee as Gadgets stepped out of the jeep. "Take Schwarz back to the base. I'm going up the hill."

Pardee guffawed, slapped the side of the jeep as it pulled away. He watched the taillights streak in the direction of the Monroe mansion. He laughed again. "Urgent!"

Wearing a white silk kimono splashed with patterns of red waves, Availa Monroe stood in the road. She raised her arms to stop the jeep, the headlights making the red and white silk blaze against the night. The soft desert wind flagged the silk. As he braked, Furst stared: in the wind and headlight glare, the woman looked like a saint seen in a dream. . .a beautiful girl writhing in flames, or flags, or the bloody rags of a shroud.

"Here, I want you here." She clutched at him, tried to pull him from the seat of the jeep. "Stop now. Get out and take me."

"Wait! Just—" He idled the vehicle off the asphalt a few car lengths and parked it against rocks. He jumped out, the sand soft under his feet.

Availa rushed to him, her kimono a pale fluttering around her. There were no embraces or kisses. She clawed her red lacquered nails into his fatigue shirt, dragged him down onto her. She tore the silk of the kimono aside and threw her body against him.

The sand was warm beneath them. She took him with her violent passion. In their few weeks as lovers, she had wanted more of him every time she called him. Now, her lust demanded every ounce of his force. She clutched, implored, commanded. She sneered when he tired. It drove him to anger. He beat her with his body, slamming into her as if to murder her. He did not slacken his pace or violence until she gripped him with her legs, spasmed and thrashed.

He slowed. She dug her nails into his back, hissed into his face: "Again. Again!"

Cursing her, he gave her two more climaxes before he collapsed, truly spent. He was too exhausted to look at her. The wind cooled the sweat on him as he lay in the sand. He felt raw and bloody.

Availa sat up, pulling the kimino closed. She drew a cigarette and lighter from a pocket. It wasn't to-bacco. She smoked marijuana laced with cocaine base. She took several long drags and stared up at the star-strewn night sky.

Finally, he sat up. Less than a quarter mile above them, the lights of the mansion blazed against the shadowy mountains, lightspill from the windows and patios illuminating the jagged, convoluted mountainsides and cliffs in patterns of red rock and black. Far below them, the base lights formed a pattern of brilliant points on the desert plateau. In silence broken only by the soft rush of the warm evening wind, she asked:

"Do you love me?"

Furst didn't answer. She looked at him for a moment. "Good," she said. "Now I don't have to pretend."

She leaned to him, kissed him, her mouth open, hot and fluid, scented with narcotic. "Next time bring more men."

He startled back. "What?"

"Or I will confess our love to my husband. Bring the other men, or you will know the wrath and revenge of Monroe."

9

Through the side door's Plexiglas, Lyons watched
the western horizon fade from red to violet. The
Huey bucked and shuddered as the pilots maintained
an altitude of fifty feet over the desert gorges and
plateaus. Every thermal updraft and crosswind threw
Lyons against the men on each side of him, or else
back against the bulkhead. Lyons gripped the nylon
and foam case for the M-14, and tried to keep the
equipment of the other mercenaries from bumping
the Starlite scope.

A man touched a lighter flame to a cigarette.
Pardee's shout tore through the engine's roar:

"Put that out before I shoot at it!"

The smoker threw the cigarette down, ground it
out. Pardee leaned to Lyons, spoke with his head
touching Lyons'.

"A night op, so what do they do? They smoke!
Two months I've nursed these losers. I should have
recruited Girl Scouts."

Time went slowly. As the sky darkened to night,
the terrain below them became black. The pilot took
the helicopter higher. Now the swerves and lurches
came infrequently. Twinkling lights appeared to the
east, then the dark form of a mountain obsured the

town. The monotonous vibration and night landscape lulled Lyons almost to sleep.

He had not slept since he'd seen Robert Furst, ex-army officer, ex-movie actor, ex-bank robber. After the gut-twisting near confrontation on the rifle range, Lyons and Pardee had returned to camp. They fitted the Starlite scope and a bipod onto an M-14, then Pardee made an unauthorized entry into the PX and carried out two six-packs of beer. Out in the hills, they drank the beer, then shot the cans to zero the rifle. Finally back in the barrack, Lyons had lain awake until dawn, figuring angles. How long could he avoid Furst? Could he risk Furst "disappearing"? Where did Furst sleep? How could Lyons get the body past the sentries?

If Lyons wanted to live, if he wanted Blancanales and Gadgets to live, Furst had to meet with a fatal accident. But how? After brooding all night, Lyons knew he could do nothing, the guarantees were too slender. Therefore he had to avoid Furst until an opportunity for elimination arose later.

The men participating in the raid had had no duties during the day. At dawn, Lyons borrowed a set of high-powered binoculars. Telling the sentries he wanted to practice, he took the binoculars and the M-14 into the rocky hills overlooking the base. Until assembly time, he studied the camp, watching the sentries, noting the frequency of their patrols and when the shifts changed. He watched the camp operations. He watched jeeps and trucks shuttle between the airfield and the base.

At four in the afternoon, he returned to the barracks and gathered his equipment. Only the crowding and the confusion in the trucks and helicopters saved him from discovery. Furst and Monroe watched from a limousine as Pardee and the squad leaders checked details and counted soldiers. Lyons had hoped Furst would accompany the strike force.... Furst would not have returned. But the man had stayed in the limousine, and waved as the helicopters lifted away.

For a moment after the helicopter touched down and the pilot killed the engine, there was silence and stillness. The rotor-throb of the other helicopters came and faded too. Pardee left his seat beside Lyons and squatted with his back to the closed side door.

"Listen up. There's no going back, you men. We're two hours into Mexico, and the helicopters have fifteen minutes of fuel left. Either we win, or we die, or we go to Mexican prisons. Right now we're going to take a walk. No talking, no noise, no smoking, no slack. When we get there, everything dies. Men, women, babies, pet lizards. You hear me?"

The squad mumbled its answer. Pardee threw open the side door and stepped smartly out. Red-lensed lights flashed from the three other helicopters. As the soldiers filed out of the Huey, cool desert air displaced the odors of fuel and sweat and face-blacking with the fragrance of chaparral and wild spices.

Lyons followed the others out. To the east, the silhouette of a mountain cut into the dome of stars. There was a very faint glow of light behind one ridge.

The glow came from the lights of the phony oil exploration airfield that concealed the doper base.

The squads formed into four lines. Then they moved. One squad took positions around the helicopters, the other three squads started the five-hour march over the mountain.

After a half-hour of stumbling through the dark, the soldier behind him jabbing Lyons every few minutes with the flash suppressor of his M-16, Lyons decided to volunteer to walk point. He jogged forward to find Pardee in the point squad.

"Do us all a favor," he grunted. "Let me and Marchardo take point."

"The dopers might have heard the helicopters—there could be an ambush up there."

"I think it'd be safer up front. Besides, if there is an ambush or there are guards up there, Marchardo and I have got a better chance than the rest of your stumblebums—"

Pardee chuckled. "They're not my soldiers. Furst hired them."

"Is it too late to trade them in on Boy Scouts?"

"Give your rifle to someone to carry. Here." Pardee pressed a weapon and bandoleer of magazines into Lyons' hands.

By touch, Lyons identified the weapon as a MAC-10 with a suppressor. He slipped out the magazine, felt the first cartridge: .45-caliber hollow point. "This'll put the hurt on someone. But I'll carry the rifle too. It might get lost."

"Great. Get Marchardo, take the point." Pardee sent Lyons forward with a slap on the back.

Moving silently up the path, Lyons found Blancanales at the head of the column, already walking point with a map and a penlight. "Let's go, brother. You do the talking, I'll do the shooting."

They moved fast, advancing a few hundred yards, then one of them staying forward while the other backtracked to the column. Lyons enjoyed the time alone. As they gained altitude, the panorama of hills, plateaus, and light-sequined desert expanded. An evening wind, carrying the scents of brush and desert soil, cooled him. He became part of the night, the distinction of where his skin touched the darkness fading, his breathing only an eddy of wind within the wind, his movement on the mountainside a mere shifting of shadows.

Leaving the clankings and rustlings of the column far behind him, Lyons continued up the trail. A pale sliver of moon rose above the mountain. Grinning to himself, he suppressed an urge to whistle. He wanted to laugh, to sing, to shatter the night and silence with his joy.

Then he smelled something. The stale odor of many cigarettes. Freezing, he sniffed the wind, listened. He dropped to a squat and crept forward. A few yards ahead, the trail went over a rise, then crossed a gravel road. Crouching there, he noted the slope beneath him to the road and the steep hill on the other side.

A metallic clink broke the silence. Lyons heard water slosh in a canteen. Someone cleared his throat, then the clink came again.

Lyons eased back. He squat-walked back twenty

yards, the MAC-10 pointed into the darkness. Then he moved fast, walking as quickly as he could without betraying himself. A hundred yards down the mountainside, Blancanales' hand stopped him.

"What's the rush?"

"Ambush up there."

They returned to the column, told Pardee. "You sure?"

"Postive. We could go around it, but I say we go up with knives and silencers. If we can get a prisoner, we can rush the top. Otherwise, it's crawl along looking for booby traps and more ambushes."

"All right, Morgan. You volunteering?"

"Me and you and Marchardo could do it."

Leading the other two men up the mountain, Lyons left the trail a hundred yards from the gravel road. Crawling on their bellies along a rabbit track, they kept a rise between them and the ambush. They crept across the road. In the brush again, they searched for a trail or animal track paralleling the road. They could not find one. They crawled again, staying high on the mountainside.

Pardee stopped Lyons. Lyons stopped Blancanales. Below them, voices muttered in Spanish. A penlight flashed on a map. The sudden squawk of a walkie-talkie broke the silence. Blancanales crept down the slope. Pardee and Lyons waited.

They heard a grunt, then thrashing. Silence. A voice called out softly in Spanish. Another voice answered in Spanish. Silence returned.

A pebble hit Lyons' arm. "Hssst!" A second pebble bounced off Lyons. Lyons nudged Pardee. They went down the slope.

In dry grass and rocks, Blancanales lay next to a Mexican gunman, his knife at the gunman's throat and his hand over the man's mouth. Blancanales motioned them close, whispered:

"This'll be my game. He's told me there's three more out there. Sit on him while I take them. If I throw a rock, it means I've got another prisoner and I want you to—"

"We've got one," Pardee interrupted. "No more. Use your Spanish, then kill them."

Blancanales hesitated. "Whatever." Then he slithered through the weeds.

Thumbing forward the MAC-10's safety, Lyons touched the bolt to make sure it was back, then kept his trigger finger alongside the guard.

Ten yards away there were whispers. A soft laugh. They heard only a quick gasp when the man died. Blancanales returned five long minutes later.

"Like he said," Blancanales muttered. He kept his voice low, but no longer whispered.

"We need to make time," Pardee told Blancanales. "Put the questions to him."

Blancanales spoke in quiet Spanish. The gunman answered questions without hesitation.

"They thought we were the Mexican Army, coming in to lean on the gang for another few hundred thousand. He says they've got two or three other ambushes on the mountain, plus booby traps. A total of ten or twelve men out here. Another twenty up at the airfield. He'll lead us up if we'll let him live."

"Sure," Pardee replied. "Promise him anything."

At the end of a twenty-foot rope, the bound and

gagged gunman led the column the last few miles to
gang base. On a rise overlooking the landing strip,
Pardee halted the column.

He cut the gunman's throat, then called his squad
leaders together.

"Mr. Morgan is our sniper," Pardee said, pointing
at Lyons. "He will shoot from this hill. Stock-
man—" Pardee gave his binoculars to a squad leader
"—one of your men will stay to spot for our shooter.
Marchardo and I and squad number one are going to
improvise a little surprise. We're going in the front
door. You others take your places. Everything as
planned. Go."

As squads two and three crept down the hillside to
their positions, Pardee briefed squad one. "Marchardo here's got real talent. He's going to take us
through the front door. If things go right, we'll get
most of the dopers before we need to use the grenades. But keep those things ready. Move fast and
kill everything. Ready, Marchardo?"

Blancanales nodded. Pardee took up the MAC-10
that he had loaned Lyons. With a mock salute to
Lyons and his spotter, Pardee led Blancanales and
the squad toward the gang's buildings.

"I'm Carl Morgan," Lyons said, extending his
hand to his spotter.

"Jimmy Lee Payne." A tall, square-shouldered
black man no older than twenty-one or twenty-two,
Payne pumped Lyons' hand like a long-lost friend.
"You're tight with Captain Pardee, right? Never
heard him call anyone Mister, not even old man
Monroe."

"We get along." Lyons nodded downhill. "Put the glasses on those buildings down there. We got maybe ten minutes to get very familiar with our targets."

While Payne studied the doper installation through the binoculars, Lyons slipped the M-14 from its case, extended the bipod legs, and scanned the buildings through the Starlite scope.

The gravel airstrip ran north to south. Approximately midpoint on the east side of the strip, there was an old adobe and rock ranch house. A patio opened to the airstrip. At the north end, several pre-fab steel hangars, much like those at the Monroe mercenary base, obviously housed planes and trucks. Behind the hangars, there were fuel tanks. Lyons spotted a sentry pacing near one of the hangars, used the man's height to estimate the distance. Three hundred and fifty yards. Judging by the height of the patio doors, the ranch house was only two hundred and fifty yards away.

After the firing started, Lyons waited. Muzzle flashes lit the interior of the ranch house.

Men from the hangars started a dash across the landing strip. Bursts from squad two on the south end of the strip dropped the men.

Automatic weapons fired wild from the hangars, spraying the darkness. Through the Starlite, Lyons saw the soldiers of squad three creep up to the rear of the hangars. Several bursts inside the buildings ended all resistance there.

The sharp crack of grenades came from the ranch house. Windows exploded outward in a white light. Several gunmen ran from the house.

Two men threw open a car's doors, died on the front seat as Lyons squeezed off two rounds to kill them, two more to disable the car. Another man sprinted across the strip, automatic fire throwing up dust all around him. Lyons put a round through the man's chest. Even as he fell, other riflemen targeted on him, several bursts tossing the man into a death-spin.

"You got a man up against the patio wall," Payne told him. "Think he's trying to—"

Lyons fired. "He *was* trying to get to that car."

Brass showered Lyons as Payne sprayed a magazine from his M-16 into the night behind them. When the action locked back, Payne dropped the rifle, threw a grenade. Before the grenade exploded, he had a second grenade in his hand, the pin already pulled free. He let the lever fly. "One, two, three, four—"

An instant before the grenade exploded, Payne threw it. Bits of steel wire showered them. But the airburst had shredded the brush thirty yards behind them. They heard a low moaning. Payne grinned to Lyons: "Think I got 'em."

Below, the firing died away. Lyons' hand-radio buzzed. "All over down here. What was that shooting up there?"

"I don't know. Payne handled it. Blew them away. The man is qualified."

"Don't waste any time up there. I'm calling the helicopters right now," crackled Pardee.

"Time to go," Lyons told Payne. They gathered up their equipment and hurried down the hill.

"Thanks for saying the good things to Captain Pardee," Payne said. "A commendation to Captain Pardee really makes my night." Payne skipped a step, slapped the stock of his M-16. "Oh, yeah, makes me feel *good*. They pay thousand-dollar bonuses in this army."

Lyons was up, too. Combat alongside this open-hearted youth had made him think back on Flor.

Now there was *qualified*.

He was happy to give young Payne a boost, but right now Lyons was concentrating his nicer feelings on that fine woman from their Caribbean cover caper.

He recalled her cold commands, her warm curves. Unlike these mercenaries, Flor was a free-lancer on the right side.

He and his spotter, Payne, descended through the brush in the darkness. He brooded for the last time about Flor. As Señora Meza, she worked her undercover skills promiscuously, drug deals here, mercenary recruitment there.... It was through her work alone that Able had connected with Pardee's intelligence people in the hellseas of the Caribbean.

Qualified for sure. And so nice to the touch. Trouble is, damn near every one of Flor's assignments featured fireballs of hijack and retribution, as Able Team had learned only too well.

Maybe, just maybe, thought Lyons, I'm better off on dry land. And he thought no more about her, put her aside for some future mission.

Now it was back to Texas. To a war with men.

10

"These men were excellent." Pardee told Furst as he pointed to Schwarz and Blancanales. "Without Morgan and Marchardo, we would've hit three different ambushes on our way up the hill. And without Schwarz's—what were they?"

"Tricks," Gadgets told him. "Electronic Counter Measures."

"—we wouldn't have come back."

"I monitored the Mexicans," Furst nodded in the gloom of the barrack. "They're totally mystified. Now, excuse us, soldiers. Captain Pardee and myself must brief Mr. Monroe."

"Wait. I want bonuses for them. They earned it."

"Then let's go talk with the man with the money." Furst saluted as he walked away.

"You'll get your money," Pardee called back to them as he followed Furst. "Count on a thousand each."

Blancanales motioned to Lyons that all was clear for him to emerge from his hiding place beneath a bundle of blankets and tarpaulin. "How're your nerves, Mr. Morgan?"

"Burned." Lyons exhaled, shuddered. "Five years ago, Furst screamed straight in my face that I was dead pork. Said he'd come back and assassinate me. And here I am. Oh, man, do I have a problem. I am giving serious consideration to going AWOL."

Lyons watched Pardee and Furst get in the limousine.

"Then again," Lyons said to his friends, "the solution to my problem is obvious. Mr. Movie Star Mercenary has got to go."

Wearing the lurid colors of a tourist—powder blue polyester slacks, a blue and green and red Hawaiian shirt, and a red L.A. Dodgers baseball cap—Bob Paxton left the air terminal and limped to the nearest taxi. The porter followed with his luggage.

All around them, groups of tourists talked and laughed and argued in American and European languages. Under the tropical sun, the airport's landscape was ablaze with the luscious colors of Jamaica's North Shore. Brightly painted hotel buses lined the curbs, drivers calling out for passengers. As if he were also a tourist, curious about a new country, Paxton stared at the crowds.

But he was not a curious tourist. He spotted Lieutenant Navarro several taxis away, elegant in his pomaded hair and waist-hugging double-breasted suit. The lieutenant saw him also, and turned away.

Paxton gave the elderly porter three crisp American dollars, then slid into the taxi. He told the driver the name of his hotel. He let himself relax, enjoying the afternoon warmth as the taxi eased through the airport's traffic jam.

Tonight, he would resume his search for the three

federal agents. He had followed them from Bolivia. A sharp-eyed, high-priced prostitute working one of the hotels in La Paz had seen two of the unidentified agents escort a husband-and-wife team of Colombian drug dealers to a limousine. The limousine had parked for an hour among the private planes at the airport. A chartered jet had flown the group to the Colombian port of Barranquilla.

Three days and thousands of American dollars in bribes later, he learned of the Colombian dealers' escape from a hijacking attempt. Within the hour, Paxton and Lieutenant Navarro left for Mexico, where they would take a flight to Jamaica.

Paxton no longer doubted the identities of the three gunmen. What better way to infiltrate the drug gangs? They would pose as mercenaries, serve with the various gangs, then betray the gangs to the same secret agency that had devastated the Mafia organizations in the United States.

El Negro put no limit on the cost of Paxton's search. The Bolivian warlord knew the legalities restricting the operations of the Drug Enforcement Agency. And he knew the danger of an agency accountable to no laws. He wanted Paxton and Navarro to find and identify the members of the new agency before the Americans imperiled his entire organization.

And then the Americans would die.

11

Leaving the singing and shouting of the raiders' victory party behind him, Gadgets left the barrack and hurried down the asphalt road. He took the last gulp from the champagne bottle he was clutching, then threw it into the mess hall's dumpster. He didn't have time for good times. With the success of three simple radar-knockout devices in Mexico, Furst had given him the task of manufacturing a full spectrum of far more sophisticated devices.

With the assignment came his own workshop, tools, materials. Passing the repair shop where he fabricated his "tricks" the night before, Gadgets went to the storeroom now appropriated as his workshop. Inside, he returned to the preliminary chores of arranging the table, the component racks and the extension cords. After setting up, he started work.

Effortlessly he assembled sub-components. He used no schematics. He worked from memory, sometimes improvising, like a musician improvising on a tune he has played a thousand times before. He tested the sub-components, then set them aside. From time to time he paused to scribble numbers on a lengthening list of parts needed. He noted ideas to discuss with Furst.

Gadgets waited until components completely cluttered the table before beginning the assembly of the first miniature microphone/transmitter and receiver....

Bottles and unconscious soldiers littered the barrack. The victory party had ended hours before. Some of the mercenaries slept in their bunks, some were sprawled on the floor. They had been paid very well for the raid into Mexico, but the intoxication was the immediate reward. After the all-night march, the battle, the dirt-level flight, they needed the release of alcohol.

Lyons and Blancanales had not allowed themselves such a luxury. Pardee had asked Commander Furst to pay the three newcomers a bonus. If Furst came with the money, and discovered Lyons—the ex-LAPD cop who had sent Furst to prison—Lyons would die. Like the other federal agents, he would be interrogated with drugs and torture, then staked out in the desert or burned alive. And Blancanales and Gadgets would more than likely die with him.

After Gadgets left early in the day, Blancanales and Lyons alternated watching the road in front of the barracks. Despite the raid, the training for the other mercenary units continued. This left the base empty during the day.

If Lyons went elsewhere in the camp, he risked Furst's spotting him. If he went into the hills again, he risked the suspicion of the other soldiers. Why did the newcomer avoid the others? Why did the newcomer hide in the desert?

He had to stay with his comrades, celebrating the perfect strike against the Mexican heroin gang. Lyons and Blancanales even pretended to drink and stagger and sing like the others.

Long after dark, Blancanales heard the car stop outside. He glanced through the door, saw Furst leave a Mercedes four-door sedan. Blancanales kicked a stack of beer bottles to alert Lyons. But Lyons was not at his bunk.

Blancanales hurried to the common washroom at the far end of the long barrack. He glanced inside, saw a soldier passed out in a shower stall, but no Lyons. Could he have gone outside? Blancanales rushed to the back door, checked the back steps. No one, only scattered bottles.

"Marchardo!" Furst called out. The athletic, immaculately groomed ex-con wove through the party's debris. He motioned for Blancanales to join him.

Blancanales faked drunkenness as he staggered to his commander. Watching him, Furst smiled, then put his arm over the middle-aged man's strong shoulders and walked him back to his bunk.

Furst sat on an empty bunk. "Looks like there was a celebration here."

"Sure was." As Blancanales fell back on his own bunk, he hit his head on the steel frame. He straightened up, blinking, rubbing the back of his head. "Had a lot to drink, had a lot to sing...." Blancanales sang a line from *South Pacific*: "...'but what ain't we got? We ain't got no dames.'"

"Maybe next week," Furst laughed. "You men

deserved whatever rewards you wanted. But security, you understand. We can't risk—"

"We could make an airborne assault on Juarez. Raid the red-light district. Get us some female conscripts."

"Wait another week," Furst told him. He slipped something from his pocket, handed it to Blancanales. "Then buy yourself a very special dame."

It was a thousand-dollar bill. Blancanales grinned, sniffed it. "This is my bonus?"

"Pardee briefed me on your role." Furst glanced around, lowered his voice. "I want to assure you, in the coming mission, that you will be rewarded in direct proportion to your participation. And I don't mean medals or combat ribbons. I mean money. Pardee told me he wished he'd recruited a hundred of you. And if he could have found good men, first-quality warriors like you and your friends, we would have paid. In this army, we do not concern ourselves with economy. Only with quality. So where's the shooter—what's his name? Morgan?"

Blancanales laughed. "Last time I saw him, he had a fifth in each hand, and was heading for the mountains. Raving like a lunatic."

"Tell him to report to my office in the morning. I'll have his money for him. And the other man, Luther Schwarz?"

"Haven't seen him in a long while. Said he had work to do. Said you gave him a promotion."

"And I also have a promotion for his bank account." Furst saluted as he left. *"Buenas noches,* Marchardo."

After Furst's boots went down the steps, Lyons came out from under the bunk.

"You were under the—?"

"Nah, man. I'm up in the hills, screaming at the moon." Lyons slipped a sheathed bayonet from under his bunk's mattress. "This hide-and-seek with Mr. Movie Star has got to quit. See you soon."

Silently leaving the barrack, Lyons saw the Mercedes parked in the road. Furst wasn't in it. A hundred yards away, in the direction of the camp's mess hall and offices, was Furst, barely visible. Lyons followed the man, staying in the shadows, yet not attempting to conceal himself. If someone saw him out of a window, Lyons would be just another soldier walking. He hoped Furst did not turn around.

Furst went to the one office where the lights were on.

As an afterthought, Gadgets added a self-switching interlock for a cassette recorder to the receiver. Once he planted the miniature microphone/transmitter, he could not expect to continuously monitor the conversations. He did not have the recorder yet, so he added cassette players to his list of needed components. He would have to dream up some device that used a tape-delay transmission in order to justify the recorder.

Looking around at the stacked components in the makeshift workshop, he thought of his own workshop back at Stony Man Farm. There, he had everything. No project was beyond his means. And if he

lacked a component or tool or instrument, he only
had to make a call. One time he'd been tinkering with
a Soviet radar unit recovered from a Hindu gunship
downed in Afghanistan. He needed a miniature
socket wrench for a crazy Russian bolt. He called one
of the numbers. Minutes later, an air force sergeant
stepped out of a helicopter with the wrench. At four
in the morning. That was good service.

Here, he had only needle-nosed pliers, micro-
screwdrivers, a soldering gun. For components he
had to scavenge parts from broken-down video
systems, aircraft transceivers, all sorts of discarded electronic gizmos. Everyone had always told
Gadgets he was inventive, resourceful, a genius, a
wizard. This job in the Texas desert proved it. He
wondered what kind of life he would have had if he'd
stuck to trade school after the army. Most likely a
job in a factory. Maybe a promotion to design or
quality control. Maybe even a college degree on the
company plan. All that driving to work in the morning. Driving home at night. Staring at a television. Wow, it made his Able Team work look like a
spell in Paradise! Even if he did get shot at sometimes.

Boots scraped on the steel steps. Gadgets shoved
the crude mini-mike and receiver into the table's clutter as Commander Furst opened the door.

"Don't you sleep?" Furst asked him.

"What? Yeah, I—what time is it?"

Furst glanced at his platinum Rolex. "After ten."

"At night?" Gadgets looked past Furst. Moonlight bathed the distant desert hills. "Oh, yeah.

Guess I lost track of time. I thought I'd get straight to work on the ECM's.''

Unsnapping the hip pocket flap of his tailored uniform, Furst took out a fist-sized roll of bills and pulled one off. He laid it on the table in front of Gadgets. "Payday."

"Gee, I don't see a lot of these. They're out of circulation, but still legal tender." Gadgets held it up to the light, snapped the crisp paper. "Grover Cleveland, my favorite president!"

While Gadgets laughed, Furst stripped off another bill and laid it on the table. Another thousand dollars.

"That for Marchardo? Morgan?"

"You. I need a favor."

His laughter gone, Gadgets waited. There was only one chair in the small room. Furst pushed aside assembled components and sat on the edge of the table.

"You seem to be able to do anything with electronics. Can you make miniature transmitters? Bugs? And a receiver?"

"Ah...sure. If I can get the parts. I don't have the parts here."

"So you go to El Paso tomorrow."

Lyons waited, invisible in a shadow, for some minutes before realizing his mistake.

Moving fast, Lyons returned to the barrack. He glanced at the Mercedes en route. Other than some dust on the tires, the luxury sedan was immaculate. Furst could not have come from the outside.

He was on his way out. Lyons went into the barrack.

"Hey, you still awake?" Lyons whispered to Blancanales.

"You do it?"

"Not yet. I think he's leaving the camp. Therefore I am going to be an uninvited hitchhiker."

"I'll stand by. Adios."

Snatching a dark blanket from one of the bunks, Lyons hurried outside. He tried the driver's door. Locked. Then he tried one of the back doors. It opened. With a last glance down the base road, Lyons climbed into the car and dropped down into the back seat's footwell.

The Mercedes had dark leather upholstery and black carpeting. With the dark blanket over him, Lyons hoped he would become only a shadow. He waited, watching the second hand of his luminous-dialed watch as it slowly completed circles.

Ten minutes later, he heard voices outside. The front passenger door opened, keys jingled at the driver's door. Then he identified the voices: Furst and Pardee.

"...we'll have to relieve the two squads down there in a few days," Pardee told Furst. His voice sounded slurred. "So he'd better come up with some new radar-baffling stuff. We can't keep pulling the same tricks on the Mexicans."

"I've got him working on more sophisticated devices," Furst responded as the car started up. "I'm sending him into El Paso tomorrow to get the electronics he needs. And he'll have another week—"

"You sending him in alone?"

Cramped under the blanket, Lyons felt the Mercedes slow for the speed bumps at the guard station. Pardee was drunk. The smell of alcohol-breath filled the car's interior. Through the soles of his boots, Lyons felt the faint vibration of a power window. Cool night air rushed into the Mercedes. He heard a sentry:

"Good evening, Commander. Captain Pardee."

"And to you, soldier," Furst replied. The car accelerated. They lurched over the second set of bumps, then the Mercedes gained speed on the main road. "No, he won't be going alone. I'll have one of the platoon leaders drive him into town."

"Is tonight an urgent meeting?" Pardee asked abruptly. Before Furst could answer, Pardee laughed.

"Depends on what you mean by...." Furst laughed also. "I don't know why Lopez thought it necessary to fly in tonight. Maybe he wants to give us a speech."

Both men laughed again. For minutes, they alternated between laughter and silence. Furst seemed slightly drunk also. Lyons felt the Mercedes float through the curves and dips of the road through the hills.

"When we go up there," Furst spoke carefully, without humor, "we need to control what the old man says around Lopez. All his talk about war with Mexico must stop. God help us if Monroe talks about nuking the country."

"Why? You think that pompous wetback will call it off?"

"I don't worry about that. It only means less of Monroe's money in my account. What bothers me is, if we panic Lopez, he could turn us in to the Feds—American and Mexican federals."

"We'll kill him."

"Won't keep us out of prison. What we really need is Monroe's doctor at the meetings. To give the old man an injection when he starts raving."

The conversation turned to jokes and laughter again. Soon the Mercedes stopped for another guard post. Sentries greeted the mercenary officers. Inside the estate, they parked the car and left.

Lyons waited a full two minutes before chancing a look. He saw the Spanish-style hacienda, its white stucco and red tiles lit by floodlights. Sprinklers swept over the landscaping of lawn and lush flowers, the water sprays like silver feathers against the desert night. Behind the car, the driveway led to the guard post. Iron gates and fence, bristling with spikes, enclosed the mountaintop estate.

To one side of the driveway was the lawn. To the other side, a high hedge. The driveway forked, the other branch going behind the hedge, perhaps to a garage.

Draping the dark blanket over his khaki and rust-splotched camouflage uniform, Lyons opened the car door and crept out. He closed the door silently, and as nonchalantly as he could he walked for the shadows of the hedge.

He smelled the marijuana too late. A sentry was crouched behind the hedge, sneaking a smoke. Seeing Lyons, the sentry startled, grabbed for the M-16 lay-ing at his feet. Lyons kicked the dopey soldier in the throat, crushing his windpipe. He wadded up the blanket, pressed it to the thrashing soldier's face as the man choked to death.

"Oh, man," Lyons muttered. "This is very bad."

Maybe tonight, maybe tomorrow, the leaders of the mercenary army would know another spy had infiltrated their operation.

12

Lyons had not intended to infiltrate the estate of Tate Monroe. Yet there he was. He would take the opportunity to learn what he could. But first he had a dead sentry to hide.

Dragging the body under the hedge, he covered it with the dark blanket. It became only a black form within the black. Lyons knew if the other guards searched with lights, or in daylight, they would find the dead man. He had to delay that discovery.

With the rifle, flashlight, and keys of the sentry, Lyons followed the hedge toward the rear of the estate. He stayed in the shadows. He waited, listened, then silently walked forward another few yards.

He came to the garage. A wide, lit asphalt area separated the end of the hedge from the doors of the garages. Behind the garage, the lawn and gardens sloped away to the iron fence, then to the rocky hillsides below the estate.

Thirty yards behind him, the rear windows of the hacienda looked out over lawns and flower gardens. Trees blocked the view of the garage. Lyons doubted anyone could see him from the house.

But there was an apartment above the garage. At

one side, stairs led to the second floor. Several curtained windows overlooked the asphalt. Curtains flagged in one open window.

Lyons slung the M-16 over his left shoulder and hooked his thumb through the sling. Letting the flashlight dangle from his right hand, he ambled across the asphalt, looking neither to the right nor left, only at his feet. When he gained the shadows of the garage, he snapped into action, setting down the rifle and slipping out his bayonet.

First he went to the garage side door. He inched it open. He heard nothing inside the building, saw only darkness. He eased inside, and closed the door silently. He waited. Listened.

Footsteps creaked on the floor above him. He heard a scrape, then more steps. Faint voices and music came through the quiet.

The voices and music alternated. Then came the sounds of shots, squealing tires, and screams. The music rose to a steady beat.... A television.

Cupping his hand over the flashlight, Lyons switched it on, his fingers tinting the glow a faint pink. He saw several limousines, a Porsche, and racks of tools. He went to the limos, tried some of the doors. The doors opened. He went to the workbenches to search for the keys to the limousines' trunks.

There was a television monitor on the workbench. A video cassette deck sat next to it. Wires connected the two. Lyons swept the area with his finger-shaded flashlight. Across from the television and tape deck, he saw a lounge chair and a five-gallon oil can. On

the oil can was an ashtray heaped with cigarette
butts, both tobacco and marijuana.

Lyons knew where he would hide the dead sentry.

A hundred youthful Tate Monroes looked down
from the walls of the trophy room. The old chair-
bound man that they had become pointed a skeletal
finger at Jorge Lopez, raved:

"You would have doubted us every step of the
way! You doubted that I could finance your coup
d'etat. You doubted I could form a secret army. You
doubted that my technicians could create the weapons, that my soldiers would have the discipline! And
on every point I, Tate Monroe, have proved your
doubts groundless. Now you demand proof that we
are capable of the strike—"

"Mr. Monroe, sir. Sir!" Commander Furst interrupted his employer. "Please, sir, don't—"

"Don't what! *What*?"

"Your anger is justified, but unnecessary. Señor
Lopez believes a command performance is required
to demonstrate our men and machines. Please see it
from his viewpoint. We have done the impossible.
Formed and trained a secret army capable of striking
deep into his nation. After all, his soldiers couldn't
do it. Correct, Señor Lopez?"

Lopez scratched at his notepad with his pen. He
considered the question for a moment before answering. "You misunderstand my request in two ways.
One, I do not doubt the ability of your force. I
viewed the films of training. I know the attack will
be devastating and deadly. I simply said that the time

of the attack approaches, and that our leader—my leader and your ally, correct me—would like to watch a rehearsal—"

"He'd risk everything, he'd—" Monroe's words were cut off by a choking fit. He coughed up a wad of mucous and spat it out on the floor. "Coming up here would risk everything! What if he were detected? What if an informer reported to your government?"

"Mr. Monroe," Lopez countered patiently. "What greater risk could El Rojo take than to go ahead without a rehearsal? The visit and demonstration would require only a day. He would come as I have come, in darkness and leave in darkness. He and the other generals would watch the demonstration, then return to their garrisons, confident of victory."

"What other generals?" Furst asked. Now it was his turn to be visibly disturbed.

"Other patriots who have the courage to stand against the wave of socialism threatening our hemisphere—"

"I'm sure they're patriots. But how many patriots do you have involved in this venture? It used to be only El Rojo's troops. Now there are more generals?"

"They are vital to the success of the coup. General Montoya heads the section responsible for all communication—the facilities, the equipment, the soldiers guarding the communications. Without telecommunications on our side, there can be no announcement of victory!"

"And the others?" Furst pressed.

"General Leon, Commander of the Paratroopers securing the Federal District. It is his soldiers who should respond to our attack. If they do not respond, we have the victory. You see, if we had to fight these forces, the socialists and leftists and communists would have time to rally their troops. . . ."

"And what about all the other generals?" Furst continued his questioning. "Will we be presenting demonstrations for them? How many generals are there? Maybe we should set up bleachers."

"We must have allies in this," Lopez told him, ignoring the sarcasm. "Your force will make the first strike, but that will not assure the victory. We must neutralize the opposition. The participation of Generals Montoya and Leon will remove the greatest threats before they can rise. Really, gentlemen, why should loyal Mexican soldiers die? With the control of the communications and the paratroopers guarding the capital, victory will be ours the very minute that your force strikes—"

Lyons heard all this outside the window. He glanced at his watch. Only another two minutes before flames engulfed the garage.

Inside the room, Lopez finally flared: "These small arguments waste time! The time of the attack nears and we—"

Forcing himself to slip away, Lyons pushed through the wet branches and flowers of the landscaping. He stayed low, using every shadow. He avoided the rectangles of light spilling from the windows. From time to time he stopped, frozen in shadow, to watch and listen.

A hundred yards away, the guards at the gate talked and laughed. To the rear of the mansion, boots paced the walkways. Lyons crept along the side of the mansion, finally coming to the hedge screening the service driveway.

Lyons straightened the rifle slung on his shoulder. He checked his uniform. To his satisfaction, he looked like a sentry. He stood in the shadow of the hedge, waiting for the flames.

He waited to the count of one hundred before glancing at his watch. In the garage, Lyons had set the video deck's automatic timer to turn on the recorder. Opening the unit, he had disconnected the power wires to the drive motor, pulled the wires out and crossed the bare ends. Then he'd put the wires into a gasoline-soaked rag, piled other rags around the video deck, and spilled gasoline on the workbench and floor. The second the timer powered the deck's motor, the short-circuiting wires would ignite the gasoline, and then the garage. Thus the dead sentry, who lay stripped of his uniform in the lounge chair in front of the television, would be unrecognizably charred.

Fire should have burst out two minutes before. But Lyons saw no flames, heard no alarms.

"Bander!" a voice called out.

Lyons pressed back into the thick branches of the hedge. He prayed he could not be seen.

A sentry walked past him, calling out: "Bander! Report to the shack!"

Waiting until he saw no sentries, Lyons stepped out of the shadows and walked leisurely across the grounds. He left the lights of the house, driveways, garage far behind him. When only ten yards of open lawn separated him from the iron fence, Lyons dropped flat beside a row of flowers and waited again.

Everywhere on the estate, he heard voices calling for "Bander!"

Lyons set down his rifle and flashlight and crawled toward the fence. He felt ahead of him, searching by touch for dips or irregularities in the lawn's turf that would indicate pressure-sensors. His hands found nothing unusual. But when he neared the fence, his ears told him that climbing the iron fence meant death.

The fence hummed with AC current. By moonlight, he examined the ironwork for wires. He found a second line of security—bundles of tiny plastic tubes that lined the upper surfaces of the horizontal cross-members of the fence.

Shouts broke the quiet. On the driveway, a sentry snatched a hand-radio from his belt, listened, then ran in the direction of the garage. More shouts came from the garage.

Lyons needed a way out of the estate, quick.

A buzzer interrupted the last part of the meeting in the trophy room. Monroe clutched the phone with a shaky hand: "What?" The old man listened for a moment, then passed the phone to Furst.

"Commander Furst here."

"Commander, someone killed Bander, one of the sentries. We found his body in the garage."

The tall, handsome mercenary resisted his first impulse: set the alarms screaming, then call for a hundred men to search the estate and hills beyond the fence. He stroked his styled hair, glanced to Lopez.

"Commander! Do you understand?"

"Yes, I heard. There can be no disturbance now." He turned away from Lopez and hissed: "We have a guest here. Keep it low key, please, for five minutes."

Hanging up, Furst turned back to Lopez. "Your plane is refueled and ready. If we have finally come to an agreement—"

"Yes, I must return. It is possible to schedule the demonstration? There are no problems?"

Both Furst and Pardee looked to Monroe. The old man dismissed the request with a wave of a bony claw. "Whenever it is convenient for my soldiers."

"Very good." Lopez gathered his notes and placed them in his leather-and-gold attaché case. Standing, he smoothed the wrinkles from his London-tailored suit. Then he leaned down to the wheelchair to shake Monroe's hand: "Until then, *señor*."

Monroe ignored the offered hand. Furst lunged forward to cover the insult, shaking Lopez's hand, putting his other hand on the shoulder of the Mexican.

"Let's get you on that plane, Jorge. Every minute we waste puts your life and our cause in danger."

Lopez glanced at the eighty-year-old man who had insulted him. "Certainly."

In the hallway, Furst walked with his arm over Lopez's shoulders. As in the trophy room, photos of Monroe dominated the walls. Also here were photos of Availa Monroe in her childhood and teenage years.

"Forget the old man," Furst consoled Lopez. "We've gotten what we need from him. And your victory will be all that he wants."

Lopez paused. "That photo. Her brother has it also. He keeps it on his desk."

It was a snapshot of Availa and her brother as teenagers, arm-in-arm. In the background, other teenage couples frolicked and embraced around a huge swimming pool. Most of the teenagers wore fashionable bathing suits. Others were naked.

"Looks like they were having a good time," Furst commented.

"...*como novios*. Excuse me, like sweethearts. They love each other so much. El Rojo will enjoy seeing her again when he comes for the presentation."

"Commander!" Availa Monroe's voice rang out in the hallway.

"Mrs. Monroe," Lopez said, bowing.

Furst only nodded as they passed. Availa moved swiftly in pursuit of them. She clutched her satin houserobe closed, following them to the entry of the mansion.

"I need to talk to you," she whispered to Furst.

"Of course, Mrs. Monroe. Allow me to take Señor Lopez to his plane. I'll return immediately."

"No! You hear me now!"

Furst opened the front door for Lopez. "Pardon

me, *señor*. Mrs. Monroe must have something urgent to tell me.''

"Of course. Good evening, *Señora*." Lopez pulled the front door closed behind him.

Availa opened her houserobe, threw her arms around Furst to enfold him in satin. She writhed her naked body against his uniform.

Furst shoved her away. "We're in the middle of an emergency."

"Then come back later. And bring other men."

"I'll send some men. But I won't be with them."

Without dropping her smile, she took her arms from him and closed her robe. *"Bueno!"*

Rushing outside, Furst saw Lopez waiting in the Mercedes. A sentry paced the driveway, rifle in hands. Furst took the soldier's hand-radio:

"This is Commander Furst. Captain Pardee is inside the house. As soon as my car clears the gate, switch on all the lights. Mobilize all the men at the base who did not participate in the Mexico raid. I want the mountain encircled while the security men search the house and grounds with dogs. Captain Pardee will direct the search until I return. Over."

Furst forced himself to walk calmly to the car. He grinned to Lopez as he entered the Mercedes and keyed the ignition. Furst idled the vehicle down the driveway to the gate. "It seems the guards are keeping Mrs. Monroe awake," he said. "They forget this is the home of their—how would you say it in Spanish? Their *patrón*?"

The guards at the gate saluted as their commander passed. Furst steered through the first curve of the descending road, then glanced in the rearview mirror.

For an instant, he thought it was the rising sun.

Sheets of flame lit the sky.

13

His ear to the smoking uniform of the soldier, Dr. Nathan heard the sucking and wheezing of fire-seared lungs. He peered at the man's face. Gasping, coughing, the man struggled to breathe, his mouth wide. The fire had charred his skin. It had blistered his eyes closed.

"Two syrettes of morphine," Dr. Nathan told the soldier who helped him with the burned man.

"No chance of an overdose?" the soldier asked as he opened the foil packets that contained the narcotic with disposable syringe.

"Doesn't matter."

Dr. Nathan crossed the asphalt to the other writhing soldier. Two sentries struggled with a fire hose, one man directing the stream of water into the garage, his helper straightening the kinks. Other sentries axed open the garage's electric doors, aimed another stream of water at the fire.

The second burned soldier thrashed and screamed under the hands of the bullnecked Captain Pardee, who held down the man's shoulders while another sentry held his feet. Dr. Nathan knelt down and pressed his ear to the man's chest. His lungs sounded good.

"How's that man over there?" Pardee asked Dr. Nathan.

"I don't think he'll make it to the hospital. His lungs are gone."

"What about this one?"

Examining the soldier, Dr. Nathan saw second-degree burns. The doctor slipped out his folding knife and cut away the man's shirt. He saw only red splotches.

"He'll live. Give him a shot of morphine, get him to a hospital with a burn ward."

"Thanks, doctor. Now why don't you go check on Mr. Monroe? All this excitement can't be good for him."

"How did this happen? What exploded?"

"Looks like someone was playing with gasoline."

"Playing with gasoline? You can't be serious."

"Into the house, doctor, please."

Two soldiers with German shepherds approached. Pardee talked quietly with them and pointed to the areas of the estate grounds unlit by any floodlights.

Dr. Nathan gave the burned man a last glance, then returned to the mansion.

In the arched entry that opened to the flower garden, Mr. and Mrs. Monroe watched the fire and the soldiers. Availa Monroe stood behind her husband's wheelchair, absently stroking the old man's thin hair.

"Pretty fire," Availa cooed, her eyes heavy-lidded.

"Were you out there, Mrs. Monroe?" Dr. Nathan asked.

She shook her head. The motion made her stagger sideways. She gripped the wheelchair, steadied herself. Monroe turned to look up at his wife. He smiled to her.

"Un momento, chiquita," Monroe joked in terrible Spanish. He looked to his doctor. "Everything under control out there?"

"Yes, sir. This has been an abrasive day for you. How are you feeling?"

"Don't concern yourself!" Monroe snapped. He smiled again. "You're right. Shouting doesn't do my heart any good. I should save my strength for important matters." The aged invalid glanced to his wife, then winked to the doctor. "What do you have to make an old man young for an hour or so?"

Availa jerked back as if she had been slapped. Her face twisted with disgust. She left the wheelchair to sit in an iron patio chair. Staring at her feet, she knotted her fingers in her hair.

"Stimulants could injure your heart, sir."

"What about stimul*ation*?" The old man leered from his wheelchair. "Availa, my dear. We go."

She struggled to her feet, lurched to the wheelchair, tried to turn it. She began to fall, only her hold on the grips keeping her upright until the doctor grabbed her hands and assisted her. They went into the house, Dr. Nathan simultaneously guiding the wheelchair and supporting the young woman.

"And for *me*," Availa whispered to the young doctor next to her. "What do you have that will make me. . .make me. . . ."

"What? Sleep? Is that why you're taking so much...medication?"

Availa smiled at him, her drug stupor gone for an instant. "It makes me far away. And that is so good. Far, far away."

Cramped in the footwell of the Mercedes, Lyons felt the doors slam closed as both Furst and the Mexican got out. He counted fifty before raising his head. Peeking out from under the blanket, he saw only darkness. He raised his head higher, saw the silhouettes of planes and helicopters against the lights of the airfield hangars. Furst and the Mexican stood near a Lear jet, the light from the cockpit and cabin windows giving Lyons a good look at the Mexican's face.

But he was no one Lyons recognized. The man's photo had not been in Stony Man's file of Latin American exiles associated with Monroe. Judging by his elegant tailoring, he was not a soldier. Lyons did not have the time to speculate.

Silently pushing open the door, he slid to the asphalt, still grasping the dead sentry's rifle and flashlight. He slung the rifle over his back and jammed the flashlight under his belt, then pulled the blanket over himself as he shimmied forward on his belly unseen. But he could not crawl and hold the blanket also, so he paused to tie the blanket's corners under his chin. Then he continued.

As his hands left the asphalt, he heard the Lear's engines whine to life. He scrambled over the gravel, finally coming to the chain link fence. Pressing himself flat under the dark blanket, he hoped he looked like a shadow.

He watched the Mexican enter the jet. Furst gave the man a wave, then returned to the Mercedes.

Lyons put his face in the dust as the car backed in an arc, the headlights sweeping over him. Lyons looked up to see the Mercedes's taillights go through the airfield gate, then accelerate up the road to the hilltop mansion.

Hills blocked Lyons' sight of the mansion, but he saw smoke rising into the night sky. Flashes lit the smoke from beneath. Fire. You could never trust cheap ignition: it had gone off, but too late. Furst would now search for the infiltrator who had killed the sentry.

Waiting until the jet taxied away, Lyons threw the blanket over the security fence's razor wire and managed to climb the chain link, squeezing between the blanket-covered coils of razor wire. In another minute, he was over the second fence. He started the two-mile run back to base.

Blancanales heard the trucks low-gearing through the base. Boots ran up the steps of other barracks. Then came shouts and the banging of steel on steel. Blancanales went out to the road, saw soldiers stumbling into the trucks. He jogged to the nearest truck.

"What's going on? Why the assembly?"

The driver leaned from the truck window. "You from Platoon One or Two? The ones that went out on last night's op?"

"Platoon One."

"Then nothing's going on, at least for you. Captain Pardee told us to haul all the other platoons up to the hill. I hear they got the dogs out."

"What're they looking for?"

"This happened before. Scuttlebutt back then was something about a federal agent. Maybe they got another one."

"Federals—"

Pushing through the gathering soldiers, Blancanales jogged to the mess hall. He turned at the crossroad and ran to the one office with a lighted window.

"Luther Schwarz!" Blancanales called out, pounding on the door.

"It's open, Mr. Marchardo."

His eyes bleary with fatigue, Gadgets looked up from his work as Blancanales rushed in. Rows of assembled components covered one end of the table. "What goes?"

Blancanales went to one knee beside Gadgets, spoke only inches from his ear. "Lyons went up the hill in Furst's car. Now they're searching the hill and the mansion. Want to go up there?"

"For sure. Ride up with me, Furst is sending a jeep."

"He is?"

"He wants me to sweep the place for electronics. I guess I know why now."

"Did he tell you anything about what happened?"

Gadgets shook his head. He left his worktable to find a cardboard box. Then he selected components and tools and filled the box. Outside, brakes squealed. A voice called out:

"Schwarz! Furst needs you up on the—"

"On my way," Gadgets shouted to the waiting driver. To Blancanales: "Come with me. Furst and Pardee trust you."

"On *our* way, *compadre*."

Mercury-arc floodlights illuminated every foot of the security fences that surrounded the base. Lyons would not risk climbing those fences. He stayed beyond the glare of the lights and moved silently through the shadows, searching for another way into the base.

He stopped to watch the activity inside. He saw lights in the barracks housing Platoons Three, Four, Five and Six. Soldiers crowded around the tailgate of a truck. Crouch-walking another twenty yards, he saw more trucks.

Search parties. First they would search the mansion and grounds, then the hill, finally this area. Lyons had to get back to his barrack before they searched the perimeter of the base.

How?

Staying beyond the light, he circled the base. He saw no openings in the fence. There was nowhere he could slide under it. Finally completing the circle, he returned to the road.

The one gate to the base stood open, the guards waving the trucks of soldiers through. Could he simply jump in one of the trucks? Join the search? No. The soldiers in the truck would question him.

Lyons lay in the rocks at the side of the road, the dust-caked blanket over him. Only a hundred yards away, the sentries talked. Occasionally he could hear a word or two.

For the next few minutes he considered the situation. Lyons knew he had been lucky. He had gone into the estate, overheard the conference, managed to get out. Also, Furst had made a mistake: he had not ordered a roll call before sending out the four platoons to search for the spy. It had not occurred to the merc commander that the spy might come from the ranks of his soldiers. Perhaps the detection of the two federal agents had lulled him to overconfidence. But Lyons could hardly count on the commander's confidence continuing through the night.

He decided he had two options. Wait until the search shifted to the area near the base, then join it and return with the soldiers to the base. Or hope for an empty truck returning to the base. But how would he know it was empty? He would have to chance that.

Flat in the roadside dust, Lyons looked at his watch. Five hours till dawn.

The jeep took Gadgets and Blancanales to the mansion's front door. They saw soldiers everywhere, some searching the grounds with flashlights and rifles, others searching with leashed dogs. Gadgets grabbed his box of tools and makeshift equipment, then went to the door with Blancanales one step behind. A soldier wielding an M-16 barred the entryway.

"At ease," Furst called, emerging from within the house. "This man has an assignment. Why are you here, Marchardo?"

"I need a helper," Gadgets replied.

"Then come in, gentlemen. What's in the box?"

"You had no detectors down in the storeroom, so I put one together." Gadgets held up a mass of wires and circuitry wrapped in black electrical tape. A nine-volt battery hung from the unit. "Doesn't look too good, but it'll find anything electronic."

"Where do we start?" Blancanales butted in.

"Okay, Marchardo, you go around the side," Furst ordered. "The men there will show you where the intruder stood under the window. Schwarz will be on the other side."

Blancanales gave the commander a quick salute and went out the front door.

Furst and Gadgets were alone in the entry hall. Furst lowered his voice to a near whisper: "I don't want Marchardo or anyone else to know why you're going to El Paso tomorrow."

"Sure, no problem."

"And after you put together what I need, you'll be coming up here to install the equipment. No one will need to know about that, either. Do we understand each other?"

"You're the head man, you give the orders."

"Good. Come on, the study's down here."

Following Furst, Gadgets scanned the rooms and doorways that they passed, trying to memorize the floor plan. Furst glanced back and saw him studying the house.

"Like what you see?"

"Where do I get mine?"

"Should see his house in Dallas. He only had this

place built so he could stay near the action. Here's the study.''

A hand-radio clipped to Furst's belt buzzed. He acknowledged the call, listened for a moment. "Be there in a minute, over. Schwarz, I want you to start near the windows. The creep could have planted something there. Then cover the entire room. When you come up to install the new equipment, I'll have you look over the rest of the house for bugs also.''

"You think someone could have slipped mikes inside the house?''

"Why not? Report to my office tomorrow when you're ready to go. If you find anything, I'll be down at the base. Later.''

As soon as the door closed behind Furst, Gadgets planted his first miniature microphone-transmitter. In another minute, he would have the room wired for stereo transmission.

The Mercedes drifted through the mountain road's curves. Pardee stared out the passenger window as if still searching for the intruder who had violated the security of the Monroe estate. Ahead of them, the taillights of the truck that carried the two burned men flashed from time to time. The hand-radio buzzed, snapping Pardee out of his thoughts.

"Captain Pardee here.''

"One of the men died. The one that was burned real bad.''

"Get the survivor to the clinic. Pick up the other set of dogs, take them to the men at the bottom of the hill. Mucho pronto.'' He put down the radio and turned to Furst. ''You heard?''

''Two dead. And a spy on the loose.''

''When I get that Fed, I'll burn him alive, I'll—''

Furst cut him off. ''Right. That's your specialty. But we still have a security problem out there somewhere.''

''We'll find him. Come daylight, he's dead.''

''But he's the third agent. Maybe this one hiked in overland. Señor Rojo should get his act together quick, because I don't think the Feds are thinking of waiting.''

''Getting shaky, Commander Furst? Don't you worry, we have a constitutional right to free assembly and the right to bear arms. Until we make the hit, the worst they can indict us for is the automatic weapons—Class Three violation. Monroe would have us out before the fingerprint ink was dry.''

''What about murder?''

''What murder?'' Pardee responded, grinning.

The Mercedes pulled up behind the truck at the gate to the base. In the glare of the headlights, they saw a soldier standing on the tailgate of the truck. Pardee slipped his Colt automatic from its holster, told Furst:

''Hit the high beams. That man wasn't there when the truck left the house.''

Pardee leaned out the passenger window and called out to the man: ''Who are you? You! ON THE TRUCK!''

The man turned to face them. Pardee eased down the hammer of his automatic, called out again.

"What're you doing out here, Morgan? Can't stay away from the action, can you?"

"I got bored!" Morgan called back.

Pardee reholstered his pistol, rolled up the window. "That's Carl Morgan, a good soldier. You met him—"

He saw Furst staring at Morgan. The handsome man's face was white. On the steering wheel, his hands were knots of tendons and white knuckles. Pardee whipped out the Colt again, jumped from the Mercedes. He pointed the .45 at Carl Lyons' face.

"Drop the rifle! And get off the truck, Morgan. Or whatever your name is, Mr. Federal Agent."

14

Squinting into the headlights, Lyons saw the Colt .45 ACP pointed at his chest. The M-16 he held had a round in the chamber. Could he flick up the safety and raise the rifle before Pardee put a .45 slug through his chest? No.

But neither would he surrender to be tortured to death. Furst had identified Lyons, his luck had run out, time to die.

"Drop the rifle, Morgan!" Pardee shouted again, the pistol steady on Lyons' chest. "Sentries! Disarm this man on the truck."

Lyons pushed up the safety. He flexed his knees, tensing his muscles to throw himself backward as the sentries reached for his rifle. He would try to spray Pardee and Furst before the sentries killed him.

A sentry started toward him, his hand reaching out to take the rifle....

"At ease, Pardee!" Furst shouted, leaving the Mercedes. "At ease! Why the hell you pointing that pistol at that man?"

"I thought...." Pardee looked from Lyons to Furst. The pistol pointed at Lyons did not waver. "When you saw him, you looked like you recognized him!"

"At ease! Lower that pistol, Pardee," Furst ordered. "You can't shoot a man simply on suspicion. Get back in the car." Easing down the hammer, Pardee jammed the Auto-Colt into its holster. Not taking his eyes from Lyons, Pardee got inside the Mercedes and slammed the door.

"Thanks, commander," shouted Lyons. "I thought I was going to get shot."

"Don't go joyriding around during a security alert! Captain Pardee has every reason to be jumpy."

In the Mercedes, Pardee watched the truck lurch over the speed bumps, Lyons clinging to the back. Pardee turned to Furst.

"Your face went white when you saw him. Why?"

"When I saw that man Morgan? I wasn't worried about Morgan. I've got my mind on something else entirely. And I can't shake it."

"What?" Pardee demanded.

The Mercedes went over the speed bumps, Furst snapping a salute to the sentries. Inside the camp, he followed the truck and saw Morgan jump from its bumper and start up the barrack steps.

"What was it, commander? What did you suddenly think of like that?"

"Did Monroe's doctor talk to you? That Dr. Nathan character asked me if Mrs. Monroe had been seen outside the house tonight. Or near the garage."

"Her? Why would he— Oh, yeah. I joked about someone playing with gasoline."

"It could have been her. It could have been her."

"Mrs. Monroe? Why would she pull a trick like—"

"Because that woman is sick. She's twisted in the head. Tonight she was so doped she couldn't stand straight. It could have been an accident, she could have done it for a thrill—"

"That doesn't explain the dead man. And when the men reported to me, they didn't mention anything about the woman being anywhere near there."

Furst stopped the car in front of the barracks where Pardee and the other officers had private rooms. Furst, as Force Commander, rated a prefab cottage with an office as well.

"Did they say how the man died? A knife? Wire or what?"

"Before I got out there, the garage exploded. They didn't—"

"Tomorrow, we question the man that lived. We might not have a spy. It might be that crazy Availa Monroe."

Still wearing his uniform and boots, Lyons sprawled on his bunk, his Colt Python near his hand. The M-16 lay on the floor, cocked and locked. He stared into the dark, every minute an eternity, waiting for Pardee to return with a group of soldiers.

He had gambled and lost. Pardee spotted him on the truck. And in the bright-as-day glare of the headlights, Furst surely recognized him as the LAPD detective who had sent the failed bank robber to prison.

But then why was he still free? Why hadn't they taken him on the spot? Did they know he would have gone down shooting rather than face torture and certain death later?

Were they watching the barrack now, waiting to grab him at an off-guard moment?

Lyons relived the scene outside the gate over and over again. A hundred yards from the gate, he had jumped on the troop truck. He was sure neither the driver nor the sentries had seen him. And the Mercedes had been on the far side of a hill. Furst and Pardee could not have seen him dash from the roadside to the bumper.

Thirty seconds after the truck stopped at the camp gate, the headlights of the Mercedes had appeared behind him. Pardee's first reaction was suspicion. Leaning out the car window, pistol in hand, he'd demanded that Lyons identify himself. But when Pardee saw it was "Morgan," Pardee joked with him, then slid back into the Mercedes and started to roll up the window.

A moment later, Pardee had jumped from the car, aiming his Colt at Lyons' chest, calling him a federal agent.

What had Furst said? One moment, Pardee joked with Lyons. The next, Pardee threatened to kill him.

The questions became a puzzle without a solution. For another hour, he replayed the scene in his mind over and over again, considering Pardee's actions and Furst's words, then straining to remember every detail of his experiences with Furst years before, in Los Angeles. He knew Furst's biography: military schools as a child and teenager; honors from an exclusive Eastern university; officer training in the army, followed by commendations and decorations in Vietnam. But then Furst had fallen apart: a bad marriage to a debutante, a boring corporate career;

squandering family money to invest in a movie starring himself; then the fast lane life with the beautiful people of Beverly Hills, including the mandatory Porsche and cocaine habit, all financed with credit and family money; finally organizing a team of drug-ruined veterans to operate internationally, but ending with a bungled bank robbery in Culver City.

Lyons laughed out loud. How could he make sense of the man's actions? Nothing Furst did made sense. Born to a good family, Furst threw it away to be a jet-set phony. Leaving prison as an ex-con with only his good looks and Vietnam record to recommend him, he became the commander of a crazy billionaire's private army.

A jeep! Voices! Lyons rolled from the bunk, grabbing the M-16. Holding the gun tight against his leg, he crept toward the rear of the barrack.

He heard the jeep accelerate away, then Blancanales' voice call out: "Thanks for the ride." Lyons reversed direction and rushed—silently—for the front entry. He stopped Blancanales and Gadgets on the front steps, without himself stepping past the doorway.

"Don't come in," he hissed.

"What?"

"Check the street for surveillance. Look around, I have to know if—"

"We already looked," Blancanales whispered. "We thought we might have people waiting for us."

"What for?"

Gadgets laughed quietly. "You don't know what we've been doing."

Lyons sighed at that. "Wait till I brief you on my adventures."

"We know all about it," Blancanales told him.

"Not the half of it you don't."

They dodged between the barracks to get to the back of a warehouse. The three of them squatted in a shadow while they exchanged stories. Lyons told them of the conference he had overheard, then the confrontation at the camp's gate. Blancanales and Gadgets told of bugging the mansion. Gadgets told them of the new assignment Furst gave him.

"Busy night," Lyons commented.

"Things are starting to pop," Gadgets added.

"Your trip to El Paso," Blancanales said, "will give us a chance to call in reinforcements."

"No chance," Lyons told him. "Mack—sorry, John Phoenix—is in the Middle East."

"Those guys in Phoenix Force *might* be available," Gadgets added. "But I don't think we need them. It's the three of us against only a hundred and fifty mercenaries.... We got them outnumbered!"

"I was thinking of Grimaldi," Blancanales told them. "All these helicopters around—"

"Yeah!" Gadgets slapped his hands together. "But we gotta come up with a plan that uses him. Maybe—"

"How can we come up with a plan," Blancanales said, "when we don't even know what's happening here? We need more information first."

"Don't you two understand what I told you?" Lyons demanded of his friends, incredulous at their scheming. "Furst spotted me. No doubt about it.

He's running some kind of scam on me. Maybe he's letting me stay free so he can watch you two. See if you're Feds."

"Makes sense," Blancanales agreed.

"Then why is he sending me to El Paso?" Gadgets insisted.

"That was before he spotted me. Maybe he'll cancel your trip. Maybe send someone else with a shopping list."

"Yeah, could be," Gadgets agreed. "So what do you want to do?"

Lyons grinned. "In the morning—which is two and a half hours from now—I'm waking up with a bad hangover. Too much booze. And the both of you and me are going to have a bad falling out...."

The next morning, Commander Furst made a call. He had the only direct telephone link from the base to the outside. Because there were no lines to this mountain base, a microwave system bridged the fifty mile gap to the nearest overland telephone lines. After he dialed the Los Angeles number, Furst gave his name to a 24-hour answering service, then spoke directly to his informant, the owner-president of a computer service company. The businessman said:

"My man Furst. Long time no talk. Is this a business or pleasure call?"

"Information."

"Business in other words. What is it you need to know?"

"Remember Detective Carl Lyons?"

The man laughed. "Bet *you* haven't forgotten."

"Find out if he's still in L.A., with the LAPD or what. If he isn't, find out where he is."

"Pay back time. Pay first, a thousand dollars."

Shots popped somewhere in the camp. Then came a burst of auto-weapon fire. Furst jumped from his seat, still holding the receiver. The telephone fell from his desk.

"—what's the noise? Someone shooting?" asked the distant voice.

"I'll wire you the money today. Call you later."

Slamming down the phone, Furst grabbed his rifle from the corner and rushed out. A soldier sprinted across the asphalt to fly up the steps in one stride.

"Who's shooting?" Furst demanded.

"Morgan! He's gone berserk!"

15

Wrestling the M-16 from Lyons' hands, Blancanales
swung the plastic-and-steel rifle like a baseball bat.
Lyons stepped back, letting the rifle stock slice past
him, then jumped forward with a kick-and-punch
combination. The kick went into Blancanales' ribs as
he back-swung the rifle, which smashed Lyons in the
arm and shoulder, and knocked him sideways onto a
bunk.

Doubled over with pain from the kick, Blancanales
could not press his attack. Lyons bounced back and
drove another kick at Blancanales. He blocked it
with the rifle, the kick bending the stock where it met
the receiver. Gasping from the pain in his ankle,
Lyons stumbled. He caught Blancanales' uniform,
slamming at his friend's face with one fist and clutching him for support with the other hand.

Blancanales spun, throwing Lyons off him. Lyons
sprawled on the floor, scrambled to get to his feet as
Blancanales swung the bent rifle overhead and
brought it down at Lyons' head. Lyons blocked the
rifle with a double-arm X block. The plastic stock
flew free, leaving Blancanales with the barrel and
receiver assembly only. He swung the shortened rifle
over his head again, and brought it savagely down.

Lyons rolled to the side so that the rifle hammered down onto the floor. It bent once more. Lurching forward, his gut hurting from the kick, Blancanales slammed the rifle down a third time. Lyons rolled safe again, but then caught the battered weapon before Blancanales could upswing. Still on the floor, Lyons hooked a foot behind Blancanales' knees and dropped him. The bent and broken rifle now in his hands, Lyons started to rise.

"What is your problem, Mr. Morgan?" Furst asked, standing over him, pointing a Colt automatic at Lyons' face.

"Kill that son of a bitch!" Blancanales roared. He held his ribs as he struggled to breathe.

"I thought you two were friends," said Furst.

Blancanales place-kicked Lyons' ribs. A soldier behind Furst rushed forward and shoved Blancanales away. Lyons groaned, choking, his arms knotted over his stomach, his knees touching his forehead. Blancanales laughed. "How's it feel? Feel good? Here comes the night!"

Lunging forward, shoving the soldier aside, Blancanales aimed a second kick for Lyons' head. Lyons rolled, taking the kick in his shoulder. The impact threw him over. Furst pointed the pistol at Blancanales' head.

"At ease, Marchardo. Take a break or I'll kill you. Soldiers!" Furst motioned to the curious soldiers crowding into the barrack. "Restrain that man. Put this other one on a bunk. Someone go for the medic."

Several men pushed Blancanales back. Some of them slapped Marchardo on the back, congratulating him on a good fight. They laughed, shoving Blancanales back when he tried to get at Lyons again. Finally Blancanales sat on a bunk, and laughed with his guards.

Two soldiers bent down to Lyons. He shrugged their hands away and rolled onto one knee. Then he stood painfully, holding his ribs, staggered to a bunk and collapsed.

Furst surveyed the damage. The M-16, incredibly, was a twisted piece of junk. Bunks lay overturned. A line of small-caliber holes stitched the enameled sheet metal of the ceiling. Two large-caliber holes deformed a wall. Trash and bottles from the previous day's and night's victory celebration littered the floor.

"What started this?" Furst asked.

Gadgets pressed through the crowd. He bled from his mouth and a bruise discolored the side of his face. "Morgan drank too much last night. He woke up drunk and hung-over, started carrying on about his wife. And then it was the politicians betraying us in Nam."

"How'd you and Marchardo get involved?"

"Marchardo told him to shut up. Morgan pulled his Magnum out, tried to pistol-whip Marchardo, I grabbed the pistol—it all went from there. Morgan acted crazy."

The camp medic arrived. "Who's hurt?"

Furst pointed at Morgan. "Give that man a twelve-hour sedative. Maybe the other one as well."

"Hey, if you're passing out pills," Gadgets joked, "me too."

"You're taking a ride to town, remember?" Furst told him in a low voice, turning away from the crowd. "I need that equipment. Tonight."

In a Kingston bar, Bob Paxton and Lieutenant Navarro waited for a Mexican. Another man had told them the Mexican might have information for them. They could do with some information. In two days and nights of crisscrossing Jamaica, passing out money and their hotel phone numbers, they had learned only that the three Americans they followed had left Jamaica in a private plane to Texas.

A hundred dollars had bought the memory of a bartender. Paxton had shown the bartender a photo of the Latin American federal agent, and the bartender remembered the Latin American meeting with a muscled scar-faced American.

Twenty dollars had prompted a doorman to remember a scar-faced man with a thick neck and strong shoulders stopping at a hotel entrance to take the three federal agents away in a rented car.

Three hundred dollars paid for three car rental agency employees to search their records and their memories. They recalled the man with the scars on his face. The records indicated that the agency had sent a driver out to an airfield to bring back a car.

At the airport, a gas-pump attendant remembered one word. A hundred-dollar bill bought that one word, "Texas." He also remembered the plane's tanks taking eighty-five gallons of fuel more than factory specifications.

A police detective came to Paxton's hotel room.

For a thousand dollars, he furnished a folder of
photos of the scarred man, and his name: Pardee.
Craig Pardee had visited Jamaica several times, the
most recent time for two weeks. He traveled with a
young blond singer. But his business was hiring
mercenaries.

This information conflicted with Paxton's reason-
ing: if the three men were federal agents, why did
they leave with Pardee as mercenaries? The United
States government did not employ mercenaries to en-
force its drug policies. But then, perhaps the contact
with Pardee was part of their cover. Or perhaps the
Drug Enforcement Agency wanted to distance itself
from the extermination of the drug gangs by using
mercenaries. Or perhaps Paxton had been wrong in
all his guesses.

The detective had also told Paxton of a group of
Mexican drug lords fleeing Mexico. Panicked, para-
noid, and wealthy, they hid in a villa outside Kingston. They were guarded by gunmen twenty-four
hours a day. One of the gunmen told of an airborne
strike by Americans on a remote smuggling base and
airfield. There had been no attempts to arrest the
gang's personnel, only a slaughter. It was this Mexican that Paxton wanted to interview. For another
thousand dollars, the detective told Paxton he would
pass on an invitation.

Now Paxton and Lieutenant Navarro waited in the
quiet bar, watching tourists wander in from the
boulevard. A sunburned brunette dropped coins in a
jukebox, selected a reggae record sung in incompre-
hensible Jamaican patois.

"Is that English?" Navarro asked Paxton in Spanish.

Paxton shook his head, glanced to the door. Two Latins stood there, scanning the interior. One man, with gray hair and a gray mustache, wore a blazing white tropical suit. The other, square shouldered and weighing over two hundred and fifty pounds, kept his right hand under his poorly cut sports coat. Paxton raised a hand to get their attention.

The Mexicans came to their table. The gray-haired man extended his hand to Paxton and Navarro. The heavy man stayed back, his right hand holding his left lapel.

"*Buenos dias*, gentlemen," the gray-haired man said. "Would you think me terribly impolite if I did not give you my name?"

"No problem, sir," Paxton answered, shaking his hand.

"First, who are you? Are you police?"

Paxton smiled, shook his head, no.

"But you ask many questions. Why?"

"Do you know of the annihilation of the American Mafia families?" Paxton asked the Mexican. The gray-haired man was clearly startled at the question. He nodded. Paxton continued. "I have sources who have kept me informed of the war against the families, the gangs, and syndicates. None of my sources could identify the vigilantes actually killing the gangs, but they did identify the federal official who was apparently in some way in charge. I had his photo in my files. Last week, we spotted this man in our country—"

"What country is that?"

Paxton smiled. He nodded to Lieutenant Navarro. "His country. The country where I live. In South America. We spotted this federal official with three agents. The official stopped at the United States Embassy, then left the country in a United States Air Force jet. But the three agents stayed.

"The agents assumed the roles of soldiers guarding two high-level drug traffickers. They left our country that night. We followed them north to Colombia, then the Caribbean, then to Kingston.

"But here, we lost them. However, we have learned two details. One is that they left with a man who the Jamaicans say is a mercenary recruiter. The other is that the agents flew to Texas with the recruiter.

"Then we learned that your camp and airfield had been attacked. We thought it might be useful to us to talk to you. Perhaps we can exchange information."

The Mexican leader stroked his mustache, studied Paxton for a few seconds. "We were attacked by soldiers two nights ago. They killed everyone who could not escape. We thought it was a raid by the Mexican army. But in my opinion it was too professional and efficient. And they spoke English."

"Could any of the men who escaped identify the Americans?" Paxton asked.

"No."

"One more question. How far from the U.S. border was your base?"

"Two hundred and fifty kilometers. That is the nearest point. It 'is approximately four hundred kilometers to El Paso. And now, no more questions. Thank you for your information. It will be of no help to us, but we know what happened at least. Good day."

The gray-haired Mexican shook their hands and promptly left the bar. His bodyguard followed him, watching Paxton and Navarro and the other patrons as he did so. Paxton laughed.

"Mexican gangsters are such a joke. They all look like politicians. And sometimes they are."

"Why did you not question them of the location of their base?" Navarro asked.

"But I did. And they told me." Paxton dropped money on the table and stood up. "Now we go to Chihuahua."

Gadgets glanced out the front window of the electronics wholesaler's shop. His driver waited in the car, still watching the shop's door. Hurrying through the shelves and racks of parts and equipment, Gadgets rushed out of the employees' entrance at the back. Three doors down the alley, he turned in through overflowing garbage cans and stacked produce crates of a Chinese restaurant.

Grinning to the cooks and waiters as he dashed through the kitchen, Gadgets stepped into the dining room. He saw a pay phone near the cash register. He paced past the tables of businessmen and housewives eating lunch. He dropped a dime in the phone. Peering through the bamboo slats screening the restaurant from the mall's parking lot, he saw his driver still waiting in the car.

He punched the phone's buttons. The operator came on the line.

"What is your billing number?"

"Don't have my charge card with me. Let me place this call collect, to a Miss Rose or anyone else who answers—"

Bent under the weight of the rocks in his backpack, Lyons marched up the trail. Sweat soaked his fatigues, and poured from his face to drip into the red dust. He turned and looked downhill. Payne—the soldier who had spotted for him on the night of the drug-base assault—trudged a hundred yards behind. Lyons rested for a moment, the afternoon wind cooling his face and fatigues. He scanned the vista below the mountains: the base and airfield, the lengthening shadows of the hills spreading across the desert, the vast horizontal planes of clouds made luminous by the sinking sun.

"Hey, Morgan! You wait!" Payne called to him.

"We're almost at the top," Lyons shouted.

"Take a break, man! I'm hurting."

Lyons found a shelf of rock where he could sit without taking off his pack or bending his legs. Awkward because of the handcuffs he wore, he loosened his packstraps. He watched tiny birds flit from rock to rock. One bird shot past, banking like a jet fighter, its belly a flash of impossible blue against the pink and red clouds of the western horizon.

Miles away, he saw a truck tow a Huey from an airfield hangar. The field crew in their safety overalls were minuscule specks of phosphorescent orange.

"Hey, Morgan! Who's on punishment march here?" Payne joked as he approached, breathing hard from the ascent of the steep trail.

"I dunno. I'm having a good time."

"Jesus. They give you some pills, then they send you out to prance around in the hills. Think *I'll* shoot up the barracks next." Payne sat on a rock and dug into his day pack.

"Look down there." Lyons pointed with his cuffed hands. "Looks like they're taking the helicopters out tonight."

"Oh, yeah. Cap'n Pardee's taking a platoon down to relieve the guys guarding that airfield down in Mexico."

"Anything going on in Mexico?"

"No one tells us anything—here!" Payne held up a beer. "Make a deal with you, Morgan. We cut off this punishment march right here, we forget making it to the top, and I'll issue half of this bottle to you."

"Might as well," Lyons shrugged. "Half of something's better than nothing."

"So Lyons is working for the Feds now?"

"That's the story," the distant voice confirmed. "Some big secret deal. You ever hear about that shoot-out on Catalina Island? Papers said some bikers freaked out?"

"Haven't had the chance to read the newspapers," Furst told his informant.

"It wasn't like the papers said. My friends in blue told me it was a major terrorist event. They took about a hundred body bags to the cooler downtown.

The night the bikers got closed down, some old friend of Lyons had a victory party. And guess who was the guest of honor?''

"Thanks a lot."

"Anytime—"

Furst hung up the telephone, picked up the camp's com-phone. He punched the code for the sentry station at the camp gate:

"This is Commander Furst. When Morgan comes in, put leg irons on him. Bring him to my office."

An hour after sunset, chains rattled on the steps to Furst's office. "Commander? We have Morgan here."

"Bring him in."

Soldiers opened the door and shoved Lyons into the office. Caked with sweat-muddied dust, sunburned, chained hand and foot, he gave Furst an awkward double-handed salute. Furst sent the sentries out with a wave of his hand.

Furst leaned back in his swivel chair, spoke softly. "Tell me, Mr. Lyons. Would it help you in your investigation and prosecution if I were to turn state's witness?"

16

Crouching in the darkness of his workshop, Gadgets twisted the steel band of his headphones. The earpieces now faced outward. He motioned to Blancanales to sit shoulder to shoulder with him.

"Now dig this."

Sharing the headphones, they listened to Furst and Pardee discuss Carl Lyons:

"...forced marched him all day. He's strong. He wore out three soldiers, but thirty or so miles calmed him down. I transferred him to other quarters, told him to avoid Marchardo if he wanted to make his money. I don't think we have any more problems."

"I want to take him south with me tonight. It'd give me time to put some questions to him."

"Why? His story checked," said Furst's voice.

"Checked too good. Everything was perfect—"

"I don't want you interrogating him."

"You're willing to risk him being an agent—"

"I don't want to risk your killing him. He's too valuable. If I suspected him at all—repeat, at all—I would have had him eliminated."

"But—"

"It's time for the helicopters to go. Leave Morgan to me. I'll have him watched."

"You interrogated Mrs. Monroe yet? Our Mexican spitfire?"

"Keep your sarcasm, Pardee!"

A tapping sounded on the door. Pushing the receiver and tape recorder and headphones into a box, Gadgets went to the door. Blancanales pressed himself to the wall behind it.

"Gadgets. . ." Lyons whispered.

"In fast!" Gadgets whipped the door open for an instant. Lyons slipped into the workshop, knocking down a box of components as he did so.

"Hey, Morgan," Blancanales hissed in the dark. "You die!"

Lyons laughed quietly. "You all right? That fight was bad."

"But realistic—"

"Shut up!" Gadgets told them. He pulled the receiver from the box. He pressed the twisted headphones to Blancanales' and Lyons' ears. "They're talking about someone named Morgan—"

"You bugged Furst's office?"

"Two minutes ago."

"Pardee's gone to Mexico," Blancanales told Gadgets. He turned to Lyons. "You missed Furst defending your loyalty. He was great."

"We've got it on the tape. I'll play it back for you."

"He'd *better* stand up for me. An hour ago, he started working for us."

"What?"

Lyons briefed them on the betrayal of Monroe's private army by its commander.

Paxton and Navarro flew from Jamaica to Mexico City, then continued to Chihuahua by executive jet. They arrived after midnight. That dawn, they left once more, in a rented Piper. Paxton directed the pilot to an isolated area of the mountains.

"*Señor*, what are we looking for?" the pilot asked Paxton. A slow man with a knowing smile, he glanced to the map his American client spread out.

"Stolen aircraft. There's an airstrip up in the mountains that's used by the oil-research teams. The thieves might be parking the planes there."

"Oh, yes. Stolen airplanes. Yes, yes. Many stolen airplanes. The drug gangs use them. Perhaps you are also looking for the drug gangs?"

"Why would I do that?" Paxton asked him. "I am paid to recover planes. Even if I found the gangs, what would be the profit? That is the business of your government."

The pilot shook his head. "It is the business of my government *not* to find the gangs!"

They laughed. Navarro leaned forward from the back seats. "How are you certain of that airfield?"

"I've been there. And if there's nothing there anymore, we'll check out three other airstrips."

They crossed the desert, then flew over the foothills into the mountains. Paxton reconfirmed the compass bearings. He glanced at his watch. The pilot gained altitude while Paxton and Navarro scanned the terrain with binoculars.

"There!" Navarro pointed to a distant glint of morning light. Focusing their binoculars on the ridge, they saw a brush-dotted gravel airstrip.

Minutes later, as they neared the airstrip, they saw no planes and no activity. The knots of brush covering the airstrip indicated months without a plane landing.

"Circle it, low." Paxton said.

Banking the plane, the pilot looked down at the strip overgrown with weeds. "*Señores*, that is not right. I have a friend, a friend of a friend, who has business here sometimes. A month ago, my friend landed a plane here. There were no—"

"In those buildings!" Paxton pointed to the hangars. "Helicopters! U.S. Army Hueys!"

A bullet punched through the cabin.

Shouting into his hand-radio, Pardee sprinted across the airstrip. His men responded instantly. Some pulled the brush and piled branches away from the hangar doors, others dragged the Hueys from the hangars. Two riflemen continued firing at the Piper even as it dived low, pulling up at the last instant. It skimmed the landscape to escape the riflefire.

The helicopter's pilot got the rotors turning. Pardee leaped through the side door. He slung his M-16 over his back and moved into the door gunner's seat. As the other soldiers filled the Huey's interior, Pardee checked the swivel-mounted M-60.

Rotor blast blew the cut-brush camouflage away, creating an open circle in the midst of the "overgrown" airfield. Dust clouded around the helicopter, then the earth dropped away and the hangars and landing strip revolved beneath them. The second helicopter lifted away.

Pardee spotted the plane. He flipped up the M-60's rear sight and jerked back the cocking lever to chamber the first .308 round. "Close on them!" he told the pilot. "Come up on their left side."

The helicopter gained on the small plane. The Piper dived, zigzagged. The helicopter closed to four hundred yards. Pardee squinted through the rear sight, fired a burst, not bothering with the elevation adjustment. Soldiers leaned against their safety straps to fire their M-16s. Hot brass flew everywhere.

"Save your ammunition, jerk-offs!" Pardee screamed at them. He saw the plane soar upward. Guessing at the distance, Pardee fired, holding the trigger back. He followed the climb of the Piper, saw sparkling glass fall from the plane. He still held the trigger back until the M-60's belt kinked, jamming the weapon. As he pulled the belt straight, he saw the Piper dive, wings wobbling.

Smoke trailed from the small plane's engine cowling. The helicopter closed to within a hundred yards as the plane straightened out. Then veered. Pardee saw a flat stretch of desert ahead. The Piper dropped its flaps to lose speed. It would land on the open stretch.

Pardee flicked up the M-60's safety. He turned to his soldiers. "Ready for some good times? We're going to have some prisoners to play with!"

Paxton smelled gasoline and excrement. Numb with shock, he pushed at the weight against him. His hands sank into something flesh-hot. He opened his eyes for the first time since seizing control of the stricken plane and landing it in textbook perfection, his breath held throughout. He found himself looking directly into the empty skull of the pilot. Three-zero-eight slugs had taken away half the man's head, exposing the sinuses and membranes of the skull's interior, as if for some medical display. The sprayed brain clotted on Paxton.

Shoving the horror away, he turned to Navarro. Jagged metal cut him. "Lieutenant. . .you alive? We got to get out. The gas tank's burst."

The helicopters roared over them. Paxton glanced out the window, saw them touching down in a storm of dust. "Lieutenant! We have to get out! The helicopters are landing. And those soldiers aren't United States Army. They'll come and finish us."

Navarro sucked air. His face was white with pain and blood loss. He cupped his hands over a gut wound. Intestines showed. His voice trembled as he spoke. "You go. I stay. I have my pistol."

His face twisting with pain, Navarro found the Browning Double-Action. Paxton took the pistol from his bloody hand.

"The first shot would ignite the gasoline."

"Then go. When they come, I shoot."

"No way, kiddo." Paxton looked down at his short leg. Shards of plastic and bent aluminum hung out of his ragged pant leg. "My phony leg's all shot to shit and I don't have a crutch. I need you for the three-legged race."

"What is a three-leg race?"

"A joke, kid. A joke." Paxton looked outside,

saw soldiers in khaki- and rust-camouflaged fatigues approaching. A voice bellowed:

"Take them alive! Alive, you hear me, jack-offs!"

Paxton recognized the voice. He turned to his wounded friend. "Hold on. I think I can work something out." Then he shouted out the window:

"Hey! Pardee! Guess who you just shot down?"

Wrapping duct tape around his shattered plastic leg, Paxton watched Pardee leaf through his notes and photos on the three federal agents. Pardee studied an eight-by-ten blow-up of the three men with Hal Brognola.

"This fourth guy is a federal? You positive?"

"Go back a few pictures—that one. That one was taken in Washington, D.C. Look on the other side, there's a photo cut out of the *Washington Post*. Read the caption. Compare the names and faces. You tell me if he's official."

"Oh, man. Have we been had."

"They infiltrated your operation?"

"Worse. The commander's covering for one of them. Don't know why, but he is."

"The commander? Who is he?"

"A candy ass named Furst. You wouldn't know him. He's never worked Latin America. Playboy warrior."

A soldier rushed into the room with a sheet of paper. He went to Paxton. "Good news, sir. Your man's going to be okay. They got him to a hospital in Madera. The doctor said he'll live through the gut wound. And the leg wound's a simple through and through. No breaks or compounds. Here's the address of the hospital and the name of the doctor.''

"Thank you—"

"Now get out," Pardee sneered at the soldier.

Paxton laughed. "Same old Pardee."

Leaving the photos, Pardee went to the broken window viewing the airstrip. "Who knows what those federals are doing up there? I can't risk flying back until after dark. And I can't risk the radio. If Furst is in it with them... well, thanks a lot, Paxton. I'm up shit-creek. But at least I know it now."

"Hang it up," Paxton suggested. "Take your men and helicopters south. I got a job for you. Thousand a week in El Salvador, popping college students who think they're revolutionaries. Easy money."

Pardee grinned, all the scars on his face standing out. "Thanks for the offer. But tonight, I give myself a promotion. Commander of the Texas Irregulars. Thousand a day, and a million-dollar bonus if I make my kill. And I always make my kill."

Even as the Mexican plane passed over the base, Gadgets finished the last of the transmitters. Each the size of a credit card, Furst studied them, held them up to the light to peer at their tiny components. He closed his hand around all five.

"I could have made them smaller," Gadgets told him. "But I just don't have the equipment here."

"Perfectly all right. You will be monitoring these until I return?"

"Yes, sir. I'll make tapes."

"Good. I have to greet our distinguished guests."

Furst gave him a quick salute, started out the door, stopped. "We are on the same team, are we not?"

"Yes, sir. Of course, sir."

"I mean, now I'm with you and Marchardo and Lyons."

"Lyons? Who is Lyons?"

Furst laughed, rushed down the steps to his Mercedes. Gadgets bolted into action. All day he had raced against the clock to finish the transmitters that Furst had requested. Now Furst had his transmitters. But Gadgets had not had the time to make the receivers. He rushed through the assembly, glancing at his watch from time to time. He needed the first receiver in only minutes, so that he could monitor Furst's conversations with the others from the first word.

Ten minutes later, he had the first unit. He slipped on his headphones and listened. He heard noises and muffled voices. "Idiot!" Gadgets muttered. "Take it out of your pocket!"

But then he realized the voices were distant to the "bug." He heard a car door slam, heard greetings in English and Spanish. Frantic, Gadgets searched through the clutter of his worktable and found a jack-cord. He tore open the package of new tape cassette recorder and jammed in some batteries. He set the cassette machine to record the conversations as he assembled other receivers, one for each miniature transmitter.

The conversations continued, in English and Spanish. They talked of "the revolution," of "freedom from socialism." They discussed careers, experiences. When one man spoke, all the others went quiet. Gadgets guessed him to be the leader of the Mexicans as the others deferred to him and called him "El Rojo," "Presidente," "jefe." He told them that his first duty upon arriving at Mr. Monroe's home was to "console his distressed sister." She had radioed to his plane, asked him to put her ahead of the affairs of state. And after all, he will be too busy the next day to visit with her. So if the gentlemen will excuse him....

Gadgets listened to the sounds of the group arriving at the Monroe estate. As they left the limousine, he heard the voice of the young Dr. Nathan:

"...forgive Mr. Monroe for not greeting you personally, but his pulse developed an irregularity earlier. So I gave him a sedative. A full night's sleep should restore him. He will greet you gentlemen tomorrow morning."

They entered the house. Availa Monroe met her brother with tears and joy and Spanish too quick for Gadgets to understand. El Rojo excused himself. His voice and his sister's faded away.

Switching on his other receivers, Gadgets heard their voices in the study. He started another cassette machine to record their Spanish. From the near-hysterical tone of Availa Monroe's voice, Gadgets thought there must be a serious problem. He heard sobbing, muffled words, and El Rojo's calm and consoling tone. Then silence.

He turned up the volume of the receiver. He strained to hear wood knock on wood, something clatter, then footsteps crossing the room. The two transmitters captured every small sound. Then he heard what he guessed to be a door bolt locking.

Continuing work on the last receiver, he listened for further conversation. There was none. But what he did hear made his hands stop their frantic work.

He heard gasping, frenzied breathing, small cries. The sounds of passionate, even violent sex.

17

Parting the plastic slats of the office's venetian blinds, Gadgets looked across the base street to his workshop. No one moved on the street. He raised the hand-radio he had purchased that afternoon, keyed the "transmit" button once, paused, then three times again quickly. It was their code for "Lyons, Gadgets calling." The hand-radio looked exactly like those issued to the sentries and platoon leaders. Gadgets had modified the three new radios to not only transmit and receive on the frequency of the mercenary radios, but also on a far-distant frequency for Able Team. Unless examined closely, the modification would not be detected. Gadgets repeated the click code.

"Holy Mother of—" Blancanales swore. Leaning over the office desk, he rewound the cassette for an instant, listened to a section again.

"They can't be brother and sister," Gadgets commented, watching the street.

"Who cares. You didn't understand any of this talk? Nothing?"

"They talked too fast for me."

"Here comes a translation," Blancanales told him. He alternated between the cassette machine's Play and Pause button, translating: "...the old man can't make love like a man...what he makes her do is disgusting...."

"Then El Rojo talks. Her sacrifice will soon be rewarded...the assassination of the President of Mexico by gringos will enrage the people of Mexico... there will be war, there will be rebellion in the barrios of the United States...the fascist gringos can't use their atomic weapons against their own cities, against a country so close to their own...in one stroke, we will create a People's Republic of Mexico and regain the territories stolen from our forefathers...."

"There it is," Blancanales concluded. "Then they make it on the floor. These people are totally off the edge, no doubt about it."

"People's Republic of Mexico?" Gadgets marveled. "A commie takeover of Mexico triggered by Americans assassinating— Oh, man. Lyons, where are you?"

"What time does Grimaldi come down?"

Gadgets glanced at his watch. That afternoon, when he spoke long-distance to Grimaldi at Stony Man, he had arranged for the ace flier to HALO (high altitude low opening) in a parachute drop on the east side of the foothills overlooking the mercenary base. He would then hike over the hills to a position near the base and wait for a signal. He would bring rations and water for three days.

"He'll be dropping any minute now," Gadgets told Blancanales. "Might even be down already. Where's Lyons? Hey, there he is."

Slipping out the door, Gadgets whistled. Lyons

jogged across the street. He followed Gadgets into the office.

"Why you over here?" he asked.

"I took this office for all my receivers," said Gadgets. "Can't have Furst walking in on this—or anybody else. Rosario, tell him what we got."

"Incest and international communism. Total mind blow." Blancanales went on to describe the taped conversation and sexual encounter.

Lyons laughed. "These people are unbelievable. But I believe it! If you ask me, I say it's time to shut this crazy camp down. We got El Rojo and his generals up there, Monroe's up there, Furst too. Any word from Grimaldi?"

"Soon," Gadgets answered. "But what about Pardee? Furst said he's the one who does the 'interrogation.' Pardee must've been the one who killed the two federals. We can't let him get away."

"Stopping the war's more important," Blancanales countered.

"The demonstration is tomorrow," Gadgets continued. "We could hijack that super-shooter Huey rocket ship, get them all at once."

They heard the throb of helicopters. The sound blasted over the base. Lyons grinned:

"The gang's all here."

Leaning against the safety strap, Pardee saw the executive jet below him on the airstrip. He shouted into the intercom:

"Pilot, don't land! Proceed to the Monroe estate. Buzz the field's radioman, connect me."

The Huey banked and left the airstrip behind.
Through the intercom's headphones, Pardee heard
the hiss of radio static.

"This is the airfield. Is there a problem, Captain
Pardee?"

"That the Mexicans' jet I saw? On the strip?"

"Yes, sir. Came in an hour ago."

"Where's Furst?"

"Commander Furst met them. They all drove to
Mr. Monroe's—"

"Pilot! Pilot—"

The radio clicked off. The pilot's voice returned.
"Yes, sir."

"Put us down in front of the house. Direct the
other pilot to land downhill, between this copter and
the security gate. And connect me to Ralston, the
platoon leader in the other copter, now!"

"Yes, sir." The channel switched. "Ralston here,
captain."

"We got a security problem at the Monroe estate.
Listen to me. Soon as we touch down, put your men
out in a half circle downhill of the Hueys. No one
fires unless we're fired on. But if anyone shoots at us,
waste them. Sentries, strangers, our soldiers, anyone—waste them. You heard me?"

"What's going on?"

"You don't need to know. Do as I told you. Over
and out."

The helicopter approached the lights crowning the
mountaintop. Pardee shouted instructions to soldiers
around him. They nodded their understanding as
they checked their rifles.

Leaves and torn flowers flew as the skids scraped the asphalt. "Shut off the engines," Pardee commanded into the intercom. He took a last glance to confirm the deployment of the soldiers from the other helicopter, then snapped himself free of his safety strap and dropped to the paving.

Furst strode from the entry with a cocktail glass in his hand. Several other men crowded from the door, Lopez in his Savile Row men's fashions and three Mexicans in dress uniforms resplendent with rows of medals and satin sashes. The tallest of the three generals, El Rojo, stood with his arm around his beautiful sister, Availa Monroe.

"What do you think you are doing, Pardee?" Furst demanded.

Driving a karate front-kick into the handsome man's gut, Pardee sent Furst flying back. He went to one knee on the choking, gagging man's chest, took the .45 from Furst's holster, slipped it into the thigh pocket of his fatigues, then pulled his bayonet. He saw the Mexicans hurrying to Furst's aid. Pardee put the bayonet to Furst's throat.

"Back up! This man betrayed us. Tell them, play-boy. Tell them about the deal with the Feds."

"I didn't—"

"You're lying! I saw the photos. All three of them, they're an elite anti-gang squad. Tell us about the deal with the Feds."

Furst gasped for breath, then screamed into Pardee's face. "I'll have you shot!"

Bending down and grabbing Furst by his styled hair, Pardee cut off his left ear. Furst screamed and wailed, thrashing under the huge man's knee. Pardee jerked Furst by the hair and slammed the back of his head into the asphalt, stunning him. He put the point of the razor-sharp bayonet to the bloody man's eye.

"You want to live, pretty boy? Tell us about the Feds! Tell us why you betrayed your soldiers!"

Sobbing like a beaten child, Furst confessed. "This is all insane, we're working for an insane old man. The Feds have already got us. For murder. For conspiracy. For—"

Grinning at the man's suffering, Pardee grabbed Furst again, this time by the throat, and lifted him from the ground. He held him at arm's length as he turned to the soldiers.

"You heard!" Pardee roared. "He's working with the FBI. He betrayed Mr. Monroe and all of you soldiers. This is a court-martial and I condemn this informer to death!"

Pardee jammed the bayonet into the struggling Furst's groin, ripped up, simultaneously emasculating him and gutting him in one long slash like he was a fish.

He dropped the dying man and watched him thrash and contort in his blood, in his spilled intestines.

Pardee wiped the bayonet on Furst's uniform and slipped it back into its sheath. Then he pulled out his .45 automatic.

"One last thing, playboy. You ain't gonna be a pretty boy in hell."

Pardee fired three times into the dying man's face.

In the dark office, they heard Pardee issue his first commands as Commander of the Texas Irregulars. "Secure the gates! No one comes or goes. Watch for Luther Schwarz, Pete Marchardo, Carl Morgan. They're federal agents. Take them alive! Pilots, start those engines. We'll be returning to the base in two minutes—"

Other voices continued, but Pardee's faded as he left the immediate area near the transmitters concealed on Furst's corpse.

Gadgets spoke into his modified hand-radio. "Can you see the camp, G-Force?"

Jack Grimaldi's voice came from the tiny speaker. "Yeah, I'm about a mile away. Hey, what's going on? About a hundred lights just came on. It's bright as day down there."

"No waiting tonight. You got here just in time."

"So what gives?"

Lyons activated his hand-radio. "Make it to the road, sir. Don't show yourself until we signal you. Move fast, situation red."

"That's what I came for. Over."

Lyons looked to Gadgets and Blancanales. "Anyone got a plan?"

"Time to get out of here," Gadgets said solemnly.

"Second the motion," Blancanales added.

"Motion carried," Lyons agreed. "Let's go get us some transportation. And equalizers."

"These false alarms have got to stop," the driver griped, revving the truck's engine. He leaned out the window to look for his helper. "Hey! Where are you?"

An arm closed around his neck. An elbow hammered into the side of his head once, twice. It smashed him into unconsciousness. Lyons opened the cab's door and dragged the driver out. He dropped the man next to his unconscious assistant. Blancanales jumped into the cab, took the wheel, continued revving the cold engine.

Lyons went to the utility compartments on the side of the truck and searched through the tools. There was the metallic rattle of chains. "All right!" He ran to the other side of the cab, took the passenger seat. "Full speed ahead."

Low-gearing through the base streets, they wove among groggy soldiers assembling outside the barracks. Blancanales and Lyons kept their faces turned away. They left the barracks and base offices behind, raced the last hundred yards to the one concrete building on the base.

Gadgets found a fist-sized rock and heaved it at the mercury-arc lamp that lit the entrance to the camp armory. The lamp shattered, sputtered for an instant, then the building went dark. The truck wheeled in a half-circle, backed up to the door.

Looping the heavy tow-chain around the bumper, Lyons dragged the chain to the door. One-inch-thick padlocked crossbolts secured the armory door to the steel door frame. A third lock switched the alarm on and off. Lyons passed the chain behind the heavy crossbolts, knotted the chain, then secured it to itself with the end hook.

"The alarm off?"

"No way, it's internal, and I can't get through the lock in less than an hour's—"

"Forget it. Turn it off when the door's open." Lyons sprinted to the side of the truck's cab, slapped the door. "Go!"

Blancanales gunned the engine and popped the clutch. The truck shot forward, lurched as the door tore free of the frame. A siren screamed.

Rushing in, Gadgets banged the light switches on, saw the wires leading from the door frame. He jammed his bayonet into the wires and tore them from the wall. The siren died. Lyons ran past him and threw a double flying kick against the storeroom door, smashing it open. He scrambled to his feet. He searched through the racks of weapons and ammunition.

Grabbing three M-203s—hybrid M-16s fitted with single-shot 40mm grenade launchers—he passed them to Gadgets. He looped bandoleers of ammunition over his shoulders. He found a case of 40mm high-explosive grenades. He also spotted a case of 40mm CN grenades and dragged them out. Gadgets returned to pick up the heavier grenade case. Lyons stopped for one more weapon: the M-14 mounted with the Starlite scope. He took the rifle and the bandoleer of .308 mags that he had loaded himself several nights before. He tried to run with the weight of the rifle and ammunition, but couldn't.

Auto-fire ripped the night. Gadgets rolled through the door, firing a burst with a silenced MAC-10 as he did so. The noise of the .45-caliber slugs ripping through the air sounded louder than the muzzle blast.

Tape on the side of the machine-pistol read "Sgt. C. Pardee."

Crouching in the doorway, Lyons felt concrete chips falling on him as 5.56mm slugs hit the armory. He shouted to Gadgets: "Cover me to the truck, then you got fifteen seconds to wire this toyshop. Make a big bang! Now!"

Slugs zipped past Lyons as he jogged for the tailgate of the truck. He rolled into the back, even as he heard slugs smashing into the truck. Then he heard the metallic report of a grenade launcher from the front of the vehicle. An explosion blasted a sheet steel building a hundred yards away.

Switching on the Starlite's power, Lyons slapped in a magazine and pointed the rifle at the shadows. The scope's electronics revealed a man's head and shoulder behind a barrel. Lyons shot him in the face. A muzzle flash betrayed another soldier. Lyons waited an instant. The soldier exposed himself as he aimed to fire again. Another head shot. A second grenade blast ripped the area. There was no more shooting.

Gadgets sprinted from the armory. "Fireworks in sixty seconds!"

"In back!" Lyons told him. As the truck started, Lyons crouched to the front of the truck canopy. He then smashed the glass out of the cab's back window. "Move it, Mr. Blancanales. Make it through that gate."

"Forget the gate!" Blancanales shouted back. Slugs ripped through the canopy's canvas and punched into the sheet metal cab. "Put out some firepower, passengers."

Lyons found the already open case of 40mm HE grenades, jammed one in an M-203. He fired wild, reloaded, fired again. He broke open the case of 40mm CN grenades. The truck swerved, throwing him on his shoulder.

Gadgets sent a blast of .45 caliber slugs through two mercenaries. The MAC-10 clicked empty. He switched magazines, but then slung the small weapon over his shoulder and grabbed an M-203, loading it with a grenade. He passed the weapon to Lyons: "Teamwork time. Just shoot."

Lyons snapped grenades in all directions as Gadgets loaded. Explosions and CN gas sent soldiers diving for cover, staggering blind and vomiting. Lyons slapped in twenty-round mags of 5.56mm, sprayed the buildings, grabbed another reloaded weapon from Gadgets, fired another grenade.

A major flash lit the night. Huge roaring shook the camp as exploding ammunition belched fire into the sky.

The truck lurched twice as Blancanales smashed through the double chain link fences, snapping off poles and shredding wire.

"We're out!"

18

Pardee charged through the stinking CN gas, snapping shots at the truck. The truck hurtled toward the road, dragging chain link and poles, disappearing into the dust clouds and darkness. A final 40mm grenade slammed into a barrack wall and the explosion ripped away the head and arms of a soldier who had been leaning there, choking on CN gas. Truncated torso and legs flopped about in the dust.

"Ralston! RALSTON!" Pardee bellowed. Holstering his .45, Pardee shoved soldiers aside, running through the confusion, searching for the platoon leader. "Ralston!"

"Here, sir!" The short wide-shouldered mercenary rushed to his commander.

"Take ten men. Get one of the helicopters to the south road. If those Feds try to make it to the state highway, hit them. Try to take them alive, but stop them."

Ralston ran in the direction of the base offices. Pardee had had the helicopter pilots land the Hueys there to speed his capture of the three federal agents, but the goddamned agents had then roared through the camp in the stolen truck.

Speaking into his hand-radio, Pardee called all his

platoon leaders: "Assemble your men. Get them into the trucks. Issue all the available ammunition. Make sure they have flashlights. Now!"

Five voices answered at once, all trying to question their new commander. Pardee cut them all off. "Shut up! Assemble your men."

The wounded screamed. Their friends clustered around the thrashing, struggling injured, wrapping field dressings over wounds, injecting morphine. Pardee saw four men gathered around one man. Two men held the sobbing, writhing man down. They spoke to console him while his other friends worked on his wounds, one of them knotting a tourniquet around the stump of a leg, the other pressing plastic sheeting over a sucking chest wound.

"Leave him!" Pardee commanded. "Assemble with your platoons."

"Sir! He's got a chance to live if—"

Pardee fired a .45 slug through the wounded man's head. "He's dead. Join your platoons."

One of the men snatched his M-16 from the dirt, tried to bring the muzzle to bear on Pardee. A .45 slug slammed him back.

"Now go!" Pardee shouted, waving the pistol past the other men's faces. Slowly, not taking their eyes from Pardee, the three men picked up their rifles, backed away, then ran toward the barracks and the waiting trucks.

Rotors throbbed. Pardee saw dust clouding against the glare of the mercury-arc lights. He holstered his Colt, ran for the second helicopter.

Jerking a tangle of chain link away from the truck cab, Jack Grimaldi swung open the door. Forty millimeter and 5.56mm brass casings fell to the asphalt. Grimaldi took the passenger seat even as the truck accelerated.

"Hey, Rosario! *Que pasa?*" The flyer extraordinaire gave Blancanales a punch in the shoulder. "Saw the fireworks down there. Anything left for me to do?"

"Sure," Blancanales grinned. "Best part is yet to come. But first, could you reload everything for me? Been kinda too busy."

"Yeah, looks that way." Grimaldi looked around at the bullet holes in the cab, the spider-web shattered windshield. He picked up the M-203, found magazines and 40mm shells.

"It's super-fly!" Lyons joked through the shattered back window.

"Ironman! When do I go to work?"

"Ever fire 106mm recoilless rifles from a Huey? A hundred of them?"

"What? Never even heard of—"

"Lyons!" Gadgets shouted from the tailgate. "Helicopter coming after us!"

Scrambling over the weapons, boxes, and rolling cartridge cases, Lyons went to the tailgate, saw the silhouette of a helicopter against the flames and smoke of the camp. But it banked to the south.

"They're going toward the highway," Lyons said. "We got them fooled."

"Guess again."

A second helicopter rose from the camp, banked

north. "Oh, shit," Lyons muttered. "Up front, prepare to get strafed!"

Grimaldi heard Lyons' warning, looked over to Blancanales. "Tell me, Rosario. How exactly does someone 'prepare to get strafed'?"

"Say your prayers," Blancanales suggested.

"No time." Grimaldi jammed extra mags for the M-203 in his jump suit's pockets. He pulled a tiny MAC-11 out of a shoulder holster, looped its strap over his right arm. He chambered a round in the M-203, opened the truck's door.

"Where you going?" Blancanales asked.

"I'm preparing to strafe back!" Grimaldi laughed as he climbed onto the roof of the truck cab. He jammed his legs down between the cab and the canvas canopy, hooked his boots through the shattered window. He braced the auto-rifle/grenade launcher on the canopy frame and waited.

Dropping down to only ten feet above the desert, the Huey paralleled the road at a hundred miles an hour.

"Pilots or the tail rotor!" Grimaldi shouted. He didn't wait for the helicopter's door gunner to fire the first round. He snapped bursts of two and three shots at the Plexiglas windshields of the Huey.

Holding the trigger down, Lyons emptied a magazine at the helicopter, dropped the empty mag, slapped in the second as .308 slugs slammed into the steel of the truck. Gadgets held the MAC-10 in his right hand, the M-203 in his left, and sprayed the helicopter, oblivious to the slugs and tracers streaking past him. Letting the machine pistol hang by its strap, Gadgets fired a 40mm grenade as the helicopter closed on them.

The grenade popped against the helicopter, releasing a puff of CN gas. "Oops, wrong box," Gadgets muttered.

As the helicopter roared past, with the door gunner firing the M-60 point-blank into the truck, Lyons sighted on the side door and fired his 40mm grenade. The flash lit Pardee's face behind the M-60, then a man crouched behind him in the interior of the Huey exploded, pieces of his body and the bodies of other men falling from the opposite side of the helicopter.

The line of tracers from the M-60 went wild, spraying the sky. On top of the truck, Grimaldi fired a 40mm HE grenade directly into the tail rotor. Steel shrieked. The tail boom disintegrated, the helicopter pitched sideways, losing the ten feet of altitude separating it from the desert. The skids hit the sand sideways, flipped the helicopter.

Rolling, rotor blades flailing the earth then breaking loose, the helicopter cartwheeled.

Blancanales didn't slow the truck. Shot through-and-through, the two right rear tires flapped against the frame. Smoke poured from the tailpipe and from under the hood. He took his sheath knife, cut the last shards of shattered windshield from the frame.

"Everybody alive?" Blancanales called out.

"We're all right," Gadgets shouted. "Where's Grimaldi?"

"I'm okay." Grimaldi, little Stony Man hero, slung his M-203 over his shoulder and climbed down from the roof of the truck. The cab's passenger seat had been shredded by .308 slugs. It smoldered from a tracer. He patted out the smoking plastic. "That was fun. But I came to fly. When do I get to do my stuff?"

"In a minute," Blancanales answered, then shouted. "Reload! Airstrip coming up!"

Accelerating, the truck lurching and bumping on its two shot-out tires, Blancanales left the road. At sixty miles an hour, he hit the chain link fence straight on. He ducked below the dash at the last instant.

Chain link and razor wire tangled on the truck's hood. Metal grinding, the truck came to a stop. Blancanales revved the engine, downshifted. The truck lurched forward a few feet, dragging wire and poles. Grimaldi leaned out the side window.

"You got a steel post jammed in the front end."

Blancanales climbed out, stepped over the tangled wire and steel, went down on his hands and knees in front of the truck. He gave the thumbs-down sign. "Time to walk."

Gadgets and Lyons gathered weapons. Gadgets paused to listen to his hand-radio, the voices frantic and chaotic. "Trucks coming. The airstrip sentries have spotted us."

"Jeep on the runway, coming this way!" Grimaldi shouted. He rested his M-203 on the truck, guessed the distance to the twin headlights, estimated the vehicle's speed, fired a 40mm HE grenade. The jeep exploded, the burning hulk rolling to a stop. "Jeep no longer coming this way!"

Loaded with weapons and ammunition, the four

men jogged toward the hangars. They saw three sets
of headlights on the road from the base. Another
jeep left the hangars, racing toward the wrecked
truck. In the center of the runway, the blasted jeep
burned.

"Quick distraction," Lyons called out to the
others. "Three high-explosive rounds, mortar-style
for the airstrip turnoff. Maybe it'll slow down those
trucks."

They braced the M-203 butt stocks against the
asphalt, fired in high arcs. Reloading, they continued
across the runway. The 40mm grenades hit without
any effect, two popping in the open desert, only one
near the road. But the trucks slowed. Gadgets flipped
the switch on his hand-radio, screamed through it to
the enemy:

"Get back, all of you! Back! We got Feds all over
the place. They're setting up a mortar. Make a run
for it. We have to surrender. They're everywhere."

For emphasis, he fired another wild 40mm round.
By some miracle, it actually hit the road, though one
hundred yards short of the first truck. Several voices
at once blared from the hand-radios.

"Not enough confusion," Gadgets grinned. "Give
me your hand-radio." He snatched Blancanales'
radio, switched it to the mercenary frequency. He set
one radio to transmit, the other to receive, put them
face to face. A high-pitched shriek filled the air. He
looped the radios together with the wrist straps.
"Until the batteries go out, nobody uses that frequency."

"Mr. Wizard strikes again!" Lyons laughed.

Spreading out to a four-man skirmish line, they rushed the hangars. Lyons saw a man run around the corner, then stop to raise his rifle. Lyons shot him. Blancanales watched the sentry station at the gate. The sentries heard the rifle shot, ducked down and aimed their rifles. Blancanales put an HE grenade into the station. There was a scream. A man crawled into the open, clutching at a twisted leg. Blancanales raised his rifle. Lyons shouted:

"Don't! Don't kill him. These guys are just ex-cons down on their luck. The Feds'll pick him up."

"Lyons the nice guy," Blancanales called back. "Can't believe it!"

A mercenary appeared in the hangar door, his hands high. "Don't shoot! I'm only a mechanic."

A second man ran out, his arms up. "We give up."

"Anyone else in there?"

"Not in there," the first man told them. "Maybe in the other hangars."

"Where's the helicopter with the 106mm rifles?" Lyons demanded.

"It's here, why—"

"You want to live? Help us get it into the air."

Motivated by Lyons' rifle, the two mechanics pushed the hangar doors wide. Grimaldi ran to the modified Huey, stared at the hundred steel tubes in the cargo area.

"This thing is deadly! Is it loaded?" Grimaldi asked the mechanics.

"Sure is! We were getting it ready for tomorrow's demonstration. Everything's tip-top."

The little man climbed into the pilot's seat.

"Demonstration happens tonight. Get this thing out in the clear."

In less than a minute, the several men hauled the Huey out to the open runway. Grimaldi started the engines. He shouted down to Lyons:

"You want to radio them? Give them a chance to surrender?"

"No talk. Just blast them. Just like they intended to do to the President of Mexico. Send their People's Republic to hell."

Blancanales laughed. "Now that's the Lyons we know and love!"

"Up, up, and away!" Grimaldi shouted over the rotor noise. He revved the engine and the helicopter floated up into the night sky.

"That's it," Lyons told the others. "This mission is hereby shut down."

"Not quite," Blancanales replied, pointing to the road. The trucks sped through the security gate, accelerated toward the hangars.

"Put grenades through the windshields!" Lyons unslung his rifle, sighted carefully, fired.

The grenade blasted the cab of the first truck. Grenades from the rifles of Blancanales and Gadgets hit the other trucks, one gutting another cab, killing the driver. The third grenade went low, exploding in the grillwork. The driver managed to swerve behind a building. The other trucks burned as soldiers scrambled from the tailgates.

Able Team didn't stop to assess the damage. Sprinting for the hangars, they sprayed one-handed bursts at the soldiers, not hitting anyone but forcing the soldiers to take cover. The soldiers returned the fire, bullets punching into sheet steel.

Inside the hangar, Lyons threw himself flat behind a forklift. Blancanales and Gadgets found cover, reloaded their weapons. Snapping a mag into his M-203, Lyons looked outside. He could see nothing.

"Mechanics! Turn off the worklights! Mechanics! Turn off—"

But their prisoners had disappeared. Lyons turned on his back, sighted on the glaring lights and shattered the bulbs with single shots. Now in darkness, they could see forms moving in the night outside, occasional muzzle-flashes.

Lyons switched on his hand-radio. The steady shriek still jammed the mercenary frequency. Lyons called across the hangar: "Gadgets! Turn off that noise! I want to try to talk them into surrendering."

In a moment, the shriek died away. Before Lyons could speak, his hand-set buzzed. It was Grimaldi:

"What's going on down there? I see fire and shooting. You want me to try out this Stalin's Organ on those trucks?"

"No. You hit the mansion. All the leaders are up there. These soldiers will give up."

"You three against how many?"

"Quality versus quantity. Hit the mansion. They'll have nothing left to fight for. Do it, flyboy."

"I'll be back quick. Over."

One of the captured mechanics had briefed Grimaldi on the rocket launcher. To the pilot's left, a black circle on the Plexiglas served as a sight. A bank of ten switches triggered the 106mm rounds in bursts of ten, the electrical trigger impulses firing at intervals of a quarter second. When the pilot hit the switch, ten rounds fired within two and a half seconds. Depending on the helicopter's speed and motion, the high-explosive warheads would strafe or saturate a target.

He circled the mountaintop estate. In the blaze of lights illuminating the grounds, he saw three men in gaudy uniforms, a man in a suit, and a woman. They stood at the Spanish-style mansion's entryway, watching the helicopter above them. Grimaldi flipped up the safety plate covering the ten switches, sighted on the entryway.

"Bye bye, People's Leaders!" he said, flipping the first switch.

His aim was a bit off. The ten rounds blasted away the second floor of the mansion, showering the generals with steel shrapnel and fragments of stucco and tile. Continuing his circle, Grimaldi saw that only the front of the house remained, the rear of the house a tangled mass of smashed masonry and framing. He sighted on what remained, flipped the second switch.

Ten more rockets blasted the house. The explosions threw the front wall over the grounds. Grimaldi circled, watching for survivors.

To his surprise, he saw one general and the woman. It was the general with the most gaudy uniform. He clutched the woman around the throat with one arm, fired a pistol at the helicopter with his other hand.

El Rojo shielded himself with his hysterical sister, put the pistol to her head. He called across the grounds to a cowering sentry:

"Radio that pilot that I will kill this woman if he does not—"

Ten almost simultaneous blasts disintegrated their bodies.

"Soldiers! Surrender!" Lyons spoke into the hand-radio. "Look up at the Monroe house. It's gone. Monroe is dead, the Mexican communists are dead. Furst is dead. Pardee's dead. There's no reason to fight. If you want to chance the desert, make a run for it. Federal officers will be here in minutes. Leave your wounded if you want. We'll see to it that they get to hospitals. There's no reason to continue fighting. It's all over. All the leaders are dead—"

An arm locked around Lyons' neck, lifted him from the concrete. Pardee's voice croaked in his ear: "Wrong, Fed. I'm alive, and you're going to die with your balls down your throat."

The ironlike arm tightened around his neck, taking away Lyons' breath, causing his blood to pound in his head. He tried to call out, couldn't. Striking out wildly, he hammered at Pardee's body of concrete, clawed at his uniform.

"Lyons?" Blancanales shouted across the hangar. "What's going on? Why—"

Unable to answer, Lyons felt his consciousness slipping away. Lights swirled in his vision as he started to die. He lashed out in a frenzy. His right hand grabbed something sticky, a wet cloth. He clutched at it, clawed.

Pardee screamed, dropped him. Lyons rolled away. A kick caught Lyons in one leg, spun him. He crawled away, gasping for air, his vision returning.

A flashlight swept the scene. Lyons saw Pardee. Smeared with blood, his face a hideous mask of contusions and hatred, Pardee swayed on his feet. Blood soaked his uniform. His right arm, the forearm wrapped in cloth and bent like a second elbow, had been strapped to his torso. In his left hand, he held a bayonet.

"Drop the knife!" Blancanales shouted.

Pardee stomped forward, going for Lyons. Blancanales fired his M-203, the two 5.56mm ultra-high velocity slugs punching holes through Pardee, spraying flesh behind him. He didn't stop. Blancanales fired again, but only one slug hit Pardee, the last round in the rifle's magazine.

"Kill him!" Lyons croaked.

Gadgets stood from cover, calmly sighted on the huge man's head, fired a burst, decapitating Pardee. He finally dropped, the razor-sharp bayonet still in his hand.

Every breath a gasp, Lyons crawled to the handradio he'd dropped. From it he heard Gadgets' voice. "That was my contribution to make up for the one-grand bonus you never got, Carl."

Lyons laughed, then pressed the transmit button.

"Everyone who can hear me! Tell your men to surrender. There's no need for you all to die. Pardee's dead. Come see for yourselves. He's dead."

It was over.

#4 Amazon Slaughter

MORE ADVENTURE COMING SOON!

Chin Pok was death incarnate. He had chosen the hunters of his private army very carefully—they were some of the most vicious hoodlums in the world.

Now he had his own plutonium factory, protected by a web of organized intrigue. There was only one way to take out Chin Pok and prevent global tragedy: Mack Bolan's Able Team!

To neutralize Pok's ghoulish scheme, Lyons, Schwarz and Blancanales probe to the core of the maniac's domain in South America—only to find blameless native slaves. Will there be a massacre of innocents before the despot could be sent to his doom?

Watch for new Able Team titles wherever paperbacks are sold

PHOENIX FORCE

AN EXECUTIONER SERIES

#3 Atlantic Scramble

ON SALE NOW!

The real Phoenix Force unleashed at last!

"Talk!" Katz spat in Arabic. "Where have you hidden the guns?"

"I don't know!" squealed the cornered killer.

"You lie!" Katz smashed him across the side of his face with the sharpened claws of his prosthetic hand. "Talk while you have a chance or I'll turn you over to *him*—" he indicated the wild-eyed McCarter, then the stony-faced Keio "—or *him*! They'll kill you by inches."

McCarter, in one swift stroke, brought up a haymaker that nearly tore the man's head off. He bore in for another shot but Yak waved him back. "Don't be greedy, David. Give somebody else a chance...!"

"Added realism and detail!"
—*Mystery News*